Raylan's brow shot up. "Your grandfather was never charged with anything, so there's technically no case to reopen. Nor was Richard Harrington ever found, so the case has fallen off the radar of the police department. Why would you want to reopen that investigation?"

"He's getting older, and he wants to clear his name before..." She couldn't say the words aloud, couldn't bear the thought of losing her beloved grandfather.

He shifted into the stiff posture of the all-business attorney he was reputed to be. The friendly, eager-to-catch-up tone disappeared from Raylan's voice. "Have you come across evidence the authorities should know about?"

"Not exactly." She thought of the file in her room back at Grandpa's, the information she'd gathered in the weeks before driving down here, the thick stack of photocopies she'd received from the Crooked Valley Police Department. Grandpa had given her the bare bones when they'd first talked a few months ago, and from there, Mia had used her resources to find more information, but no solid answers. "I want to start at the beginning and retrace everything that happened."

Raylan's gaze narrowed. "And how do I figure into this?"

Mia shifted in her seat. This was the hard part—the place where she expected Raylan to disagree or, worse, throw her out of his office. "I want you to investigate it with me."

Shirley Jump is an award-winning, *New York Times*, *Wall Street Journal*, Amazon and *USA TODAY* bestselling author who has published more than eighty books in twenty-four countries. Her books have received multiple awards and kudos from authors such as Jayne Ann Krentz, who called her books "real romance," and Jill Shalvis, who called her book "a fun, heartwarming small-town romance that you'll fall in love with." Visit her website at shirleyjump.com for author news and a booklist, and follow her on Facebook at Facebook.com/shirleyjump.author for giveaways and deep discussions about important things like chocolate and shoes.

Books by Shirley Jump

Love Inspired Cold Case

After She Vanished

Love Inspired Mountain Rescue

Refuge Up in Flames

Visit the Author Profile page
at Harlequin.com for more titles.

A GRAVE MISTAKE

SHIRLEY JUMP

LOVE INSPIRED
INSPIRATIONAL ROMANCE

LOVE INSPIRED®
INSPIRATIONAL ROMANCE

ISBN-13: 978-1-335-46844-4

A Grave Mistake

Copyright © 2023 by Shirley Kawa-Jump, LLC

This is a work of fiction. Names, characters, places and incidents are either the
product of the author's imagination or are used fictitiously. Any resemblance
to actual persons, living or dead, businesses, companies, events or locales is
entirely coincidental.

For questions and comments about the quality of this book, please contact us
at CustomerService@Harlequin.com.

Love Inspired
22 Adelaide St. West, 41st Floor
Toronto, Ontario M5H 4E3, Canada
www.LoveInspired.com

Printed in U.S.A.

Recycling programs
for this product may
not exist in your area.

Be of good courage, and he shall strengthen
your heart, all ye that hope in the Lord.
—*Psalms* 31:24

To my nana, who was one of the best storytellers
I ever met.

Chapter One

The last time Mia Beaumont put on a dress had also been the last time anyone ever asked her to wear one, and for good reason. As soon as her mother had fastened the last button, Mia scooted out the back door and climbed the oak tree in the backyard, scuffing up her new shoes and turning the lacy edge of the pink-and-white skirt into a shredded tail. Somewhere in some dusty photo album there was a picture of ten-year-old Mia, sitting on the lap of the Easter Bunny—really, it had been kind Mr. Klein from next door, dressed in a once-white costume that had seen better days—with a smudge of dirt on her cheek and fresh scrapes on both knees and one elbow. Her annoyance with the dress showed in the scowl on her face, the crossed arms over her chest. After that day, her mother had given up on trying to tame her middle daughter.

The kettle on the stove started whistling. Mia

crossed into Grandpa Louis's cramped, sunny kitchen and turned off the burner. "Grandpa, do you want some tea?"

She fixed two cups, anyway, one with milk and honey for herself and one with just a sprinkling of sugar for her grandfather. She put the mugs on a tray and added a plate of shortbread cookies. Her feet were already complaining about the heels she'd put on to go with the dress.

"Grandpa?" Mia navigated her way through a house crowded with memories and photographs. She paused by a candid shot of her mother in the coffee shop, her hair up in a bun, an apron around her waist.

For most of Mia's life, Anna Beaumont had been busy doing her level best to keep her head above water, especially back in those days. Mia's father, who was gone more than he was home, had been a commercial pilot flying for a major airline based out of Dallas. By the time Mia was fourteen, her parents were divorced, and Anna was working two jobs, both as a waitress and at the family coffee shop, so she could hold on to the little house where the three girls had grown up. As soon as Chloe, the youngest, turned eighteen, Anna took a job in Chicago managing a restaurant. The little house had been sold and the girls were on their own.

All three of the girls had taken their turns working in the coffee shop that their maternal grandmother had started with her sisters and continued to run long after most people retired. Chloe stepped in to take over full-time shortly after Grandma died, while Julia worked part-time around her occupational-therapy schedule. They'd kept the moniker of Three Sisters Grindhouse, even though only two of the Beaumont sisters worked there. By that time, Mia had been off on her own, living in New York City, scraping by as an artist and doing her best to avoid her family.

When she'd left Crooked Valley, Mia had been angry, defiant and very, very stubborn. That she'd graduated high school at all was a feat in and of itself, and when she'd piled her guitar and all her most vital belongings in the hatchback she'd bought used from Cappy Winstead, her grandmother had shaken her head and told her that one day Mia would come home, full of regret.

Well, Mia had finally come home for longer than a day or two. Her paternal grandfather, whom she adored, had called, and when Grandpa asked something of her, Mia found it impossible to say no. Especially when that request involved a mystery and especially when Grandpa said he was worried someone might be following him.

Those words had been enough for Mia to drop everything and rush across the country. She watched her grandfather sleeping and knew she would do anything for him. His eyebrows knitted together, as if he was worrying about something in his sleep. How she wished she could take that worry away.

Thirty years ago, Grandpa Louis had been a suspect in the disappearance and presumed murder of his business partner, Richard Harrington. There'd been an investigation, a threat to prosecute and a financial blow to her grandfather's business that he'd never really recovered from. He'd moved out of the investment world and into accounting, trading the career he loved for one that was a close second. For three decades, he'd never talked about the Harrington disappearance with his family. Until he'd been diagnosed with cancer and he'd realized his time to clear his name was quickly evaporating. On the anniversary of the disappearance, Grandpa Louis had done an interview with a local reporter, and three days later, he'd called Mia, convinced someone was following him.

Maybe someone was and maybe someone wasn't, but either way, Mia intended to solve this mystery once and for all, which meant calling in a favor. Hence, the dress.

Mia picked up her shoes and headed down the hall. She stopped in the bathroom and checked her reflection. Given how infrequently she wore dresses, there was a good chance she had it on inside out or something.

The dark gray poplin dress nipped at her waist, exposing tanned and toned arms and legs, both the result of hours in the gym. She grabbed a claw clip out of her makeup bag and fastened her long, curly, dark blond hair into some semblance of order. All she needed was a strand of pearls and she could have been June Cleaver's twin. Well, if the television mom from the fifties had ever played in a grunge band in New York City and spent her days hosting a YouTube channel about unsolved crimes.

Either way, Mia looked far more confident and put-together than she felt. She could do this. The past was the past. It didn't have to impact her present.

She checked on her grandfather, who was still sleeping, thankfully, and then quietly left the house. As soon as she walked outside, she stepped into a sweet, crisp, early winter breeze of fresh mountain air that slid off the Rockies and deep into Crooked Valley, a town nestled halfway between Denver and Boulder. Crooked Valley Creek ran behind her grandfather's modest ranch house, and then skirted the mountains that flanked two sides of the town, which left most of Crooked Valley lush and green for a good portion of the year while the mountains held the caps of white that attracted skiers from around the world. The morning had started out brisk, a typical late November day, then as the sun climbed over the mountains and shone through the thin air, the temps had risen to the high fifties. At night, the air would plunge into the forties again, a dichotomy that made everyone in Crooked Valley keep both a jacket and a pair of sunglasses in their car year-round.

Mia got into her CR-V, giving the Honda a mental apology for the miles it had traversed and the dust coating the wheels. On her way to her sister Chloe's house for dinner later, Mia would take a run through the car wash and bring the white crossover back to its usual shininess. For now, there was the one stop that she'd dreaded for more than a thousand miles.

She drove through downtown Crooked Valley, a long red-and-tan patchwork of brick and stucco buildings, punctuated by a view of the Rockies rising above the end of Main Street. She pulled into a space in front of city hall, shut off the car, fed a few quarters into the meter and then headed inside the imposing marble-and-stone building. A gruff security guard waved her through the metal detector and then pointed at the elevator bank after she asked for the office she needed. She rode up to the fifth floor, where she found an expansive glass office emblazoned with a Colorado state crest and a familiar name.

Office of the District Attorney
Twenty-Third Judicial District
Hugh Levine, District Attorney
Raylan Westfield, Assistant District Attorney

A dozen years ago, Raylan Westfield had been her first kiss, her first love, her first everything. He'd made her head spin and her heart race, and for a second, the wanderlust-filled Mia considered staying in Crooked Valley. Then she'd gotten a job in New York City, and it became clear they wanted two different lives. Mia had left Raylan behind, along with the collection of stuffed animals in her room and her trophy from the seventh-grade spelling bee.

Raylan had stepped into his father's shoes soon after Frank had retired a few years ago. Frank had been the DA for twenty years, and now Raylan seemed to be on the same career trajectory, if what everything Mia had heard was true. Levine was considering retiring in five more years, and Raylan was liked well enough in town to become the next DA, just like his father. From all Mia had read on the internet, Raylan was a great prosecutor, maybe even better than his father had been.

Except Raylan's father had gotten one thing wrong—there was no way Grandpa Louis had a single thing to do with the disappearance of Richard Harrington. Now all Mia had to do was prove it. Hopefully with the ADA on her side.

Mia pulled open the glass door and strode into the main office area. The glass door snicked shut behind her. Another woman might have hesitated, at the very least spent a couple of seconds gathering herself or taking a few deep breaths before seeing her ex-boyfriend. Not Mia. Everything she had to do, she tackled the same way she jumped into a chilly lake—headfirst and without hesitation.

A gray-haired woman looked up from a desk, and her face broke into a welcoming smile. "Mia?"

"Mrs. Linscott, what a surprise." Genuine warmth filled Mia's voice. "I didn't know you were working for Raylan. I thought you retired when Frank did."

Mia's old neighbor, office assistant to the former DA and sometimes weekend babysitter for the Beaumont girls, as well as the Westfield boys, waved off the words. "Keeps me out of trouble. I thought I wanted to retire, until I tried it. So I came right back here to work for Raylan when he was hired. It's like starting all over again because Raylan is just full of energy and drive." A familiar mischievous twinkle shone in her eyes and in her smile.

Mia had always liked Susan Linscott. The whole neighborhood had been friendly, the houses and families as interlaced as a spiderweb. The Linscotts had lived in a house at one end of the block, the Westfields at the other, with the Beaumont girls in the middle. When Mia's mother had to work a weekend shift and her grandparents were unavailable, Susan Linscott had filled in as babysitter. More often than not, Raylan and his little brother had been there, too, since his father worked endless hours and their mother had been sick with cancer for many years before she died. Mia and Raylan had spent so much time together as children that it seemed like them ending up together had been a foregone conclusion.

"How have you been?" Susan got up from behind the desk and drew Mia into a warm, tight hug. Estée Lauder perfume filled the air. For a moment, Mia felt like she'd come home. "How's life in New York?"

"Busy. Crowded. Gray. I'd forgotten how beautiful it is here." Mia's gaze landed on a broad landscape painting that dominated one wall of the ADA's front office and featured three different Colorado seasons. The deep terra-cotta tones of the Rockies in the autumn, winter pastels of the mountains draped in snow and a bright blue sparkling river in spring. She had missed Crooked Valley more than she realized until she'd come back to all this beauty.

"It's been so long since I saw you," Susan said. "What, ten years?"

"Twelve. I left right after I graduated high school," Mia said.

"And now...?" Susan arched a hopeful eyebrow.

"And now I'm back in Crooked Valley, but just for a little while, not forever." That was all Mia wanted to say about her plans, since she wasn't quite sure how she was going to pull off the next part. Getting Raylan to agree wasn't going to be easy. As for her sisters... well, one mountain at a time. That was how the settlers got from here to California, right? "Is Raylan in?"

Susan beamed, clearly in matchmaking mode. "He is indeed. Did you want to see him?"

Not *see him*, see him. Just get him to agree to be... open to a wild plan. And if he wasn't, she was going to go forward regardless. "Yes, but only if he's not busy. If so, I can make an appointment."

"Oh, no, he's never too busy for you." Susan picked up the phone on her desk and punched a button. "Raylan, there's someone special here to see you. You're going to be *so* surprised."

Mia tried not to roll her eyes. He was probably going to expect either Sofía Vergara or Santa after that vague description. Clearly, Susan thought there was still something between Mia and Raylan, but she was wrong about that. "I can make an appointment, Susan."

"Nonsense." Susan waved off the very idea. "He'll be thrilled to see you." She listened a second more, then nodded and agreed. After she hung up the phone, Susan came around the desk and ushered Mia toward a door a few feet away. "Oh, and before you go in there, Mia…"

"Yes?"

"Raylan's still single. Just sayin'." With that cringeworthy sentence, Susan opened the door. "Raylan! You'll never believe who's here."

Raylan Westfield rose from behind his desk, all six foot two of dark-haired, muscular, why-is-he-still-so-hot man. Mia teetered on the unfamiliar heels and began to perspire under the dress that felt made for a stranger. Half of her had hoped that Raylan was sporting a balding head and a desk paunch, but if anything, he was in better shape now than in high school. He had on a pale blue shirt with a pair of pinstriped navy pants. His floral-patterned tie was loose at the neck, giving him an almost vulnerable, cozy look. The matching suit jacket hung on a coat-tree behind his desk. His wire glasses had been traded for a pair of dark-framed lenses that offset his square jaw. He looked handsome and relaxed, all at once. A powerful combination.

So much for there being nothing between them. There was definitely still something in the air, but since Mia was good at ignoring things she didn't want to face, that something was not going to be a problem.

"Mia?" Raylan smiled. "Wow. When Susan said I'd be surprised, she wasn't kidding."

"I'm sorry for just showing up. I should have made an appointment." She turned to go, but Susan blocked the doorway. How on earth could Raylan, of all people, leave Mia feeling flustered? Mia never got flustered. *Lord, help me get through this meeting. Grandpa is counting on me.*

"I'll leave you two to catch up." Susan gave Mia a smile, then shut the door. Mia had no choice but to turn around and stay.

"Come in, come in." He waved her toward the desk. "It's nice to see you. Have a seat."

Mia sank into the soft leather visitor seat. He settled into the massive dark brown swivel chair on the other side of his thick mahogany desk. There was a mess of files on one side, a triple stack of legal pads with various scribbles in the middle, but otherwise the office was neat and tidy. Raylan's doing? Susan's? Why did Mia care? "Thank you for agreeing to see me." She put her hands in her lap and did her best to look professional. "I'm here on business, of sorts."

He chuckled. "Have you committed a crime in Crooked Valley? Because all I'm doing is prosecuting right now, and if that's the case, I'll give you the name of a good defense attorney."

"Why is that the first thing you assume about me? People change, you know, Raylan." She scowled and got to her feet. That man still managed to get on her nerves with a few words. "This will never work."

"Mia, hold on. I'm sorry. It was just a joke." He ran a hand through his hair and sighed. "Let's try this again. How have you been, Mia? I'd love to catch up with you."

The sincerity in his voice made her lower herself back into the chair, even though she was sorely tempted to bolt from the room. She reminded herself that impetuous, wild Mia was gone. More or less.

She took a deep breath. "I want to reopen my grandfather's case." Might as well get to the point sooner rather than later.

Raylan's brow shot up. A moment of silence extended between them. "I saw that interview your grandfather did, and I'm not sure why he's talking about the case now, after all these years. Your grandfather was never charged with anything so there's technically no case to reopen. Nor was Richard Harrington ever found, so the case has fallen off the radar of the police department. It's a cold case. Why would you want to reopen that investigation?"

"He's getting older, and he wants to clear his name before…" She couldn't say the words aloud, couldn't bear the thought of losing her beloved grandfather. "Anyway, it's time to do that."

He shifted into the stiff posture of the all-business attorney he was reputed to be. "Have you come across evidence that the authorities should know about?" The friendly, eager-to-catch-up tone had disappeared from Raylan's voice.

"Not exactly." She thought of the file in her room back at Grandpa's, the information she'd gathered in the weeks before driving down here, the thick stack of photocopies she'd received from the Crooked Valley Police Department after her Freedom of Information Act request last month. Grandpa had given her the bare bones when they'd first talked a few months ago, and from there, Mia had used her resources to find more information, but no solid answers. "I want to start at the beginning and retrace everything that happened."

Raylan's gaze narrowed. "And how do I figure in to this?"

Mia shifted in her seat. This was the hard part—the place where she expected Raylan to disagree or, worse, throw her out of his office. "I want you to investigate it with me."

"You...what?" He blinked. "Why me?"

"Because no one knows the history of Crooked Valley better than you do, Raylan. I haven't been here in twelve years, and frankly, I was never really fully here when I lived here, anyway. This town and I... We're not exactly bosom buddies. But you're like a walking encyclopedia, and if I'm going to go back in time thirty years, I need someone like you on my side." Raylan was also one of the smartest, most fair men she knew, and if anything Mia discovered did point to her grandfather, Raylan was the only person she trusted to investigate first and indict second. It was a gamble—a huge one—but she had no choice. Going behind the backs of the police and district attorney on a case this legendary would only make Grandpa look more suspicious, not less.

But if she got Raylan's buy-in from the beginning, maybe the real facts could be uncovered and Grandpa's name could be cleared. Maybe.

"My father thought your grandfather was guilty," Raylan said. "He just didn't have enough evidence to take the case to trial."

Raylan's father hadn't just thought Grandpa Louis was guilty. He'd shouted it from the rooftops. Frank Westfield had been a ruthless prosecutor, intent on throwing anyone he deemed guilty into jail forever. He'd called a grand jury to indict Grandpa, but thankfully the grand jury hadn't thought there was enough evidence to take the case to trial. Nevertheless, Grandpa's reputation had been destroyed forever, tarnished by a verdict that never happened. She prayed the Raylan she remembered had maintained the ethics and sense of fairness he'd somehow been born with, unlike his father.

"I know that. I was thinking maybe you'd want a little closure on it, too. For your dad. And, for old times' sake." She gave him a smile that she hoped was a bit flirty, but Mia had about as much flirt in her as she did elephant. She smoothed the skirt of the dress over her knees and wondered vaguely if Raylan thought she looked pretty. And then chastised herself for caring what he thought. The dress had been a way to butter up Raylan, maybe help him forget the past and agree to her plan.

Raylan pushed his glasses farther up the bridge of his nose. The dark-rimmed glasses served to accent the deep blue of his eyes, offset the roguish wave in his hair and draw her attention to his face, over and over again. "You know we'd be on opposite sides of this, right?"

"Would we, Raylan? Because I've known you a long time, and you've always been a fair and honest man. I know it's a risk coming here to ask for help from the assistant prosecutor, but—" and here was why she'd worn the dress and pulled out all her feminine stops, including another rare smile "—I was hoping you'd help me because we're old friends."

"Is that what we are, Mia?"

"That's the best definition I can think of." She met his gaze, but his dark eyes were like storm clouds at night—unreadable. He'd always been that way, but then again, so had she. Neither of them had been big on sharing feelings or fears, which was part of what had led to them breaking up and Mia doing what she did best—fleeing the scene of the heartbreak.

The end of their relationship might not have had a big blow-out argument, but they hadn't exactly been pen pals over the years, either. Whatever was between them was…complicated.

He leaned in and gave her an assessing gaze. "I noticed you wore a dress today. Beautiful, but not like the Mia I know."

She raised her chin and avoided looking at him. "You haven't seen me in a long time, Raylan. I have changed."

As Raylan sat back in his chair, it let out a slight squeak of protest. "Your grandfather has always been considered a person of interest in this criminal matter, and if I help you with this, I will be compelled to use any and all evidence I uncover in the course of an investigation."

"English, Raylan. Not lawyer."

He sighed. "I can't promise that I won't prosecute your grandfather at the end of this."

The idea terrified her, but Mia refused to let that stand in her way. Grandpa had been the one to propose involving Raylan, even knowing this could end up backfiring on him. Her grandfather was innocent in all that had happened. She just had to prove it. "All either of us wants is some answers. I'm willing to take that risk if you are. Do you want to solve this mystery with me or not?"

He rose and came to sit on the corner of his desk. She shifted in the chair and feigned disinterest. "Depends. You're not still holding a grudge against me, are you? Because we were just kids back then. Barely out of high school."

Her gaze met his and held. The clock on the wall ticked away the time. Outside the office, she could hear the soft murmur of Susan talking on the phone. "I don't remember. It was a million years ago."

"Liar."

She raised her chin and looked him dead in the eye. If he thought he still had any hold over her, he was wrong. She didn't feel a single blip when he smiled at her. Not a single one. "I'm serious, Raylan. I don't remember the past. I've moved on. You've moved on. The whole world has moved on."

"Of course. Who thinks about things like high-school romances, anyway?"

"Not me." The dress had been a bad idea, she decided, because it knocked her out of her element. Made her feel too much like a girl and less like herself. "So…are you in or out?"

He shook his head and laughed. "You're either incredibly foolhardy or wildly optimistic, Mia. I gotta admire you either way."

"I'm not sure whether to thank you or slug you." She gave him her sweetest, least-sarcastic smile.

He chuckled. The bemused expression still lit his eyes, as if he found her sitting in his office a clever ruse on her part to see him again. "How about dinner tonight? We can catch up."

Mia got to her feet. She might have thought about him a couple times over the past few years, but she certainly wasn't here to rekindle a dead fire. "We both said all there was to say a long time ago, Raylan. If you're going to help, then be at the Harrington property tomorrow morning bright and early. Wear boots and bring gloves. We're going to dig until we find something."

Mia left Raylan's office, kicked off her shoes and got behind the wheel of her car barefoot, despite the cold temperature. Those shoes sure had looked good in the store when she'd bought them, but in reality, they were torturous to wear.

She was about to put the car in gear when she saw something in the rearview mirror. A flash of something dark, a face maybe, but when she looked up, whatever or whoever had been behind her was gone. Mia shrugged off the goose bumps that rose on her arms and pulled out of the parking lot. She made a quick stop at the supermarket and then, a few minutes later, she arrived back at her grandfather's house. She put the shoes on again just long enough to climb up the back staircase, unlock the door and slip inside the kitchen.

Then she braced herself, because every time she saw Grandpa, it broke her heart and made her regret staying away for so long. The Grandpa Louis that Mia remembered from her childhood had aged considerably and had lost his usual perky personality. Part of it had undoubtedly been the death of his wife a few years ago, a loss they'd all been saddened by.

He'd kept working until he was seventy-eight, filling the holes in his life, he said. A month after he retired, he was diagnosed with lung cancer, and the busy, hearty grandfather she remembered had disappeared. He'd finished his last round of chemotherapy last week, and Mia prayed it had stopped the cancer from spreading.

When Mia arrived last night, she'd barely been able to hide her shock at seeing the wizened, frail man who greeted her, so changed in the year since she'd seen him. The cancer had taken pounds off his frame, weakened his muscles and left him looking perpetually tired.

After her meeting with Raylan this morning, she'd gone to Mac's Market and stocked up on all of Grandpa Louis's favorite foods. Maybe she could get him to eat some spaghetti and meatballs or a pizza tonight, or anything he wanted to order. She hoped and prayed that focusing on the case would give him motivation to work on being as healthy as possible again, so she kept her voice bright and her smile on her face.

"Hi, Grandpa! I'm back!" She left her shoes in the corner and deposited two canvas totes on the counter. A half-eaten shortbread cookie and nearly full teacup sat beside the sink. Well, at least he'd taken a couple of bites.

"I'm in here," her grandfather called back.

She ducked into the living room, where Grandpa Louis was sitting in his usual recliner, with an afghan over his legs and the remote in his hand. The blinds were drawn and the room was dark, save for the light from the television. Mia clicked on a lamp and perched on the love seat across from her grandfather.

Nothing in this room had changed in the years since Grandma died. Nothing had changed anywhere in the house. It was as if Grandpa had lost the love of his life and then stayed stuck in that moment. If Mia had known how bad it was here…

Well, there was nothing she could do about the past. All she could do was make the future better. "How was your day?"

"Exactly the same as all of them." Grandpa muted the television and shifted toward her. "Did you talk to Raylan?"

The only time she saw her grandfather perk up and become a semblance of his old self was when he talked about reopening the case. That was one area where Mia could help him. It was almost as if God had pushed her along the path she'd been on for the last few years, investigating cold cases for her YouTube channel, because now she could put all those skills to use and help bring closure to her grandfather. Her channel had focused mainly on women who were leaving domestic-violence situations, but she knew she had enough investigative chops to hopefully help solve a disappearance. If nothing else, she could at least clear Grandpa Louis's name and stop the whispers in town that said he'd had something to do with his business partner's disappearance.

"I did. He's skeptical, but I think he's going to help me."

Grandpa arched an eyebrow. "I can't imagine his father would have been happy about that, if he was still alive."

"I don't know." Mia shifted closer and put a hand on her grandfather's knee. "Either way, we'll have some answers, Grandpa, and maybe even find out where Richard went."

"And where the money went." Her grandfather scowled. "That man cost me everything. Your grandmother and I had to start over from nothing. It was a tough time."

Grandma had gone back to work as a nurse, Grandpa to a small accounting firm, and the two of them slowly rebuilt their savings, barely keeping their house from foreclosure. Mia had never been very close to her father, who traveled a lot when the girls were young, but she had spent a lot of time with her grandparents. Now that Mom was gone, Grandpa Louis and her sisters were the only thing Mia had left that resembled a family.

That connection was what had made Mia hop in her car and put her life in New York on an indefinite hold. She'd solved several mysteries over the years with her YouTube channel show, but this was the first time it was personal, and it was ten times more important because it was Grandpa's story. Now that she was here, she wanted to get right to work and lift the weight of suspicion off her grandfather's shoulders once and for all. "If you're feeling up to it today, I'd like to do a formal interview with you for my show."

Her grandfather scowled. "I'm not much for that technology thing. What if I mess it up?"

"It's just you and me talking. It'll be easy. I promise." And it would give Grandpa Louis a reason to get out of his pajamas and out of his recliner. "We can start after you have a healthy snack or an early lunch."

"You're always trying to get me to eat." Grandpa smiled and reached for her hand. "And maybe I'm not as grateful as I should be. Thank you for taking care of an old man."

"That's because you're my favorite old man ever." She gave him a hug and held on a little extra, long enough to stop the tears threatening her eyes.

An hour later, Mia made a simple lunch of tomato soup and grilled-cheese sandwiches. Grandpa tried eating, but barely got four or five bites in him. Mia pretended that didn't worry her at all as she helped her rail-thin grandfather change into a button-down shirt and sweater. She set up her ring light, phone camera and tripod, and created a vignette by moving a faux fern and a lamp into a corner of the dining room. She brought in the comfiest armchair she could find in the house and helped her grandfather ease into it. She clipped a lapel microphone to his sweater and brushed off a piece of lint. He looked so fragile and weak that all she wanted to do was hug him and never let go. "I promise to keep this short."

Grandpa Louis waved off her concern. "Take all the time you need. I just want to get to the truth."

"Okay." Mia grabbed her notebook, sat in a chair opposite her grandfather and clipped a microphone onto her own shirt. The phone's lens was set right behind her head, so that she was partially in the shot with her grandfather. She would intersperse the interview with some B-roll—footage of the town and the site of the disappearance—to give it more depth and interest. "Take me back to the beginning. How did you get involved in investing?"

Grandpa Louis chuckled, clearly happy to start with a topic he loved so much and had such a passion for. "When was I not into investing? I remember having a paper route when I was a boy. Thirty cents of every dollar I made went into a savings account. Back then you'd get an actual return on your investment from the bank. By the time I graduated high school, I had enough money saved to invest in a couple of stocks, which did pretty well, considering I didn't know what I was doing. I went to college, majored in accounting and finance and learned all I could about money. I had made friends with this guy in my fraternity, Richard Harrington. He was majoring in finance as well, and was smart as a whip. He said he knew a way to double our money." Grandpa paused, and Mia could see that the memory pained him.

"If it's too difficult to talk about, we can do this later."

"No. It's waited long enough." Grandpa shifted his weight and took a deep breath. She could see him struggle with bringing a painful past to the surface.

"I trusted Richard because he seemed to know so much more than me, and he did. We went into business together after college, and by our thirties, the company was making over a million dollars a year."

Mia let out a low whistle. "Almost three million in today's dollars."

Grandpa nodded. "And a lot of money for a couple of young men. Your grandmother and I had just started a family with the birth of your father. We were raising him in a nice neighborhood, sending him to private school, taking the occasional family vacation. We lived very well, your grandmother and I, and we were so grateful."

"How was working with Richard Harrington? Did you like him?"

Her grandfather shrugged. "Richard and I got along pretty well most of the time. He handled the operations for the business, and I managed sales and customer relations. We met weekly to discuss the investments the company was making on the clients' behalf, and I trusted that he was doing what he promised. Life was sweet…until it wasn't."

"Can you tell me what happened?" She already knew these answers, but it would be better for the show if she could get them on tape. Plus, allowing Grandpa to ramble with his memories might spark some other connection that would give her a good starting point for investigating.

"I would if I could, but I don't really know myself." Her grandfather shifted in the chair and spent a moment adjusting the blanket across his legs. "One day, Richard was here, and the next he was gone. And so was every dime the company had. Every investment people had made with us, all of our operating capital—everything was gone."

"What did you do?"

He shook his head, and tears glimmered in his eyes. Mia knew how guilty her grandfather still felt about what had happened. Richard had broken the trust of their clients and, for some of them, stolen all of their retirement money and savings.

"I hired a forensic accountant to try to find the money," Grandpa said. "I thought maybe Richard moved it offshore or something. Turns out the day before he disappeared, he transferred everything from the business into his personal account by forging my signature, since I was a cosigner. That morning, someone went to the bank and got a cashier's check. Whoever that was walked away with close to four million dollars."

"You said *someone*. Doesn't the bank know for sure who had that check drawn?"

Grandpa shook his head. "Only a few banks had cameras in those days, and the video they did get was poor quality. Whoever withdrew that money knew exactly which window to go to, because it was the only window with the view obscured by a potted plant. The teller was young and new and nervous, which is why I think that person selected her to do the transaction. She didn't remember many details.

Of course, with a transaction that large, the bank manager had to sign off on it. That day, though, the regular manager was on vacation, and a manager from a different branch was covering for him. To that man, Richard was a stranger. All he could do was compare the driver's-license image and signature with what was on the withdrawal form. The manager swears the license matched the man who made the withdrawal. And, it's Richard's signature on the withdrawal forms, too. For the most part."

"What do you mean by 'for the most part'?"

"The police think the signature was forged. Something about the way some of the letters were written seemed off to them."

That could have been due to stress, Mia knew. If Richard was under a lot of pressure to get the money, his hand might shake when he signed the forms. It could also be because the person who had withdrawn the money wasn't Richard Harrington at all. Without any high-quality video or still images, there was no way to know who went to the bank.

Mia paused before asking the next question. She hated putting her grandfather through this, but he was the one who wanted answers, and there was no way to get those without asking the hard questions. "Did the police suspect you had something to do with it? Especially because the signature was presumed to be forged?"

"Not at first. For a few days, they thought Richard had just flown the coop with all the money. I figured he was living on a beach in Mexico or something. But after they saw that signature, they came back around and asked more questions." Grandpa Louis sighed. "I had no alibi for that morning, because I was here alone at the house. Your grandmother was at work, and I had taken a sick day. I'd come down with the flu a couple days before and was at home, in bed, sick as a dog."

"But no one saw you at home at the time the money was withdrawn and can vouch for you?"

Grandpa Louis shook his head. "No." He paused. "And then there's the matter of the other money."

"What other money?" Mia had no doubt her You-Tube channel would love Grandpa Louis and feel bad for all he had been through, because her own heart went out to him every time he spoke.

"In the last couple of weeks before his disappearance, Richard seemed to become very suspicious and paranoid. He cleaned out his personal accounts, and he had a good amount of money in there, because he wasn't supporting a wife and child. He had several withdrawals over those last few weeks, somewhere close to a half a million dollars. He never told me what the money was for, but he did tell me that he had hidden his money on the property."

"He told you that?"

Grandpa nodded. "I think he wanted someone to know, in case anything ever happened." He leaned forward, staring into the camera. "He said to me,

'Louis, if anything happens to me, you need to search my house. Everything you'll need is in there.'"

Mia shook her head. She already knew from the police report that Harrington's house had been searched after the police began to wonder if Richard was dead, not on vacation. If there'd been that much money in the house, they would have found it. "That seems like an odd thing to say."

Grandpa shrugged. "I don't know if he was just talking or if he really did hide something at the house. The police searched that place top to bottom and side to side and never found any money. Maybe Richard did, as they first thought, run off to Mexico with all the money."

"But you don't think that." Mia gently probed at the reason she had come here.

"No." Her grandfather let out a long breath. "I think Richard is dead and that money is still out there."

She wanted to ask him about his theories behind Richard's possible death, but could see the exhaustion in her grandfather's features and the slump of his shoulders. She reached over and stopped the video recording on her phone. "That's enough for today. We'll cover more ground later."

"Are you sure? I can keep talking."

She wanted to come back to her grandfather with answers the next time she did an interview, not keep hammering him with painful questions. They could get to the rest later, if she could finally wrap up this mystery.

No. There was no *if*—*when* she solved it. She refused to let her poor grandfather worry for one more day.

Mia helped Grandpa Louis back to his recliner and got him settled again. Even the short interview had taxed his energy. The doctor had told them to expect some weakness after the chemotherapy treatments ended, but to Mia, it seemed like her grandfather wasn't rebounding like he normally did. Her heart worried, and her mind prayed for him to get better.

Mia gathered up her notes and told her grandfather she was heading up to her room to do some more research. "I'm going to Richard's property first thing in the morning. It's still vacant, so I'm going to poke around and see if I find anything."

"Don't go getting into trouble." Her grandfather's features filled with worry. "This family has had enough run-ins with the police. We don't need someone else ending up as a suspect."

"That won't happen. I promise." Even though she knew it wasn't a promise she could guarantee.

Chapter Two

Raylan argued with himself for the better part of the next morning, coming up with at least a dozen reasons why he shouldn't help Mia Beaumont with this investigation. At the top of the list was his own personal conflict of interest, as in Mia had once been the woman he thought he'd marry someday. As much as he wanted to think there was no trace of attraction left between them, he knew that was a lie.

The second she'd walked into his office, she'd stolen his breath. She was as beautiful today as she had been twelve years ago, maybe even more so now. She would be a distraction—something he didn't need right now. Like most ADAs, his caseload was bursting at the seams, and his personal life barely had a pulse.

He knew what his father would say—*finish what I couldn't*. Frank Westfield had been a driven, dogged prosecutor who'd left the office with a handful of cases unsolved and a reputation tarnished by a few wrong moves. Frank hadn't had enough evidence to indict Louis Beaumont thirty years ago, something that had bothered him long after he'd been forced to put in his retirement paperwork because of the Alzheimer's that robbed his memory and had eventually put him in a care home, where he barely remembered his breakfast, never mind his son.

Raylan lasted an hour at work before the curiosity and drive to have the answers his father needed pushed him out of his seat. Maybe solving this crime would be a way for him to give his father a gift. Even Raylan knew that was a long shot. Every time he visited his father, it was like having a conversation with a stranger. Raylan would bring up old cases or talk about family and friends, and there was rarely a glimmer of recognition in his father's eyes. It broke Raylan's heart to see the man he admired and emulated become a shell of himself, with all those brilliant moments erased from his mind.

There was nothing Raylan could do about the medical diagnosis, or the loss he felt when his father's mind took him away. He could only try to be the best possible ADA and, maybe someday, the best possible DA this area had ever seen and be able to continue his father's legacy of making sure justice was served.

In many ways, Raylan's motivations were the same as Mia's. They both wanted to help the people they

loved and solve the mystery. When it came to the Richard Harrington case, however, Raylan had a sinking
suspicion that those answers would very likely come
at a high cost for one of them. The real and heart-
breaking possibility that Raylan would find enough
evidence to convict Mia's grandfather loomed over
him, a storm cloud of what-ifs. He didn't want to be
the one to destroy her family, but he also didn't want
this mystery to remain unresolved for another three
decades, or let Mia wade into deep waters like these
alone. The only way to get those answers was to do
what Mia had asked…and get involved.

Raylan grabbed his jacket from the coatrack.
"Susan, can you reschedule my calls for the rest of
the morning? I have something I need to do."

"Of course." She clicked over to his schedule on
her computer. "When will you be back?"

"After lunch. This shouldn't take long." He thought
a second. "Actually, just to be safe, let's reschedule
everything for today. If there's anything critical, let
me know and I'll respond."

Susan nodded and then gave him a smile. She had
always been a beautiful woman, even well into her
sixties, with a friendly smile and bright, sparkling
blue eyes. "Does this sudden day off involve a cer-
tain Mia Beaumont?"

"Only tangentially." He held up a hand before
Susan could say anything else. He loved Susan and
her family as much as his own, but that didn't mean

he was going to rekindle his relationship with Mia just to satisfy her decades-long matchmaking efforts. "Nothing is happening or will happen between us, Susan."

Susan let out a long sigh. "Too bad. You guys were such a cute couple."

He chuckled as he slipped his arms into his coat and dug his car keys out of the pocket. "You are an incurable romantic, even after all these years working in the DA's office. I'm surprised it hasn't made you jaded."

"Hope is a good thing, Raylan. It's what makes the job mean something at the end of the day." She smiled. "I think you could do with a little of that yourself."

Raylan scoffed. "I deal with facts, not fantasies. See you later this afternoon."

The drive to the Harrington property took him through downtown Crooked Valley, past his old friend Mike Byrne's veterinary practice and later, Three Sisters Grindhouse, the coffee shop Mia's family owned. Last winter, Crooked Valley had been on guard, terrified by an arsonist who had wreaked vengeance on several residents and their businesses. Once he'd been caught, Doug Jameson pled guilty, saving the district the cost of a trial and expediting his trip to prison. That was one of those wonderful days when Raylan could see the good his office and the law-enforcement officers he worked with could do. He might not be a romantic, but he was warmed by the knowledge that one more bad guy was behind bars.

Raylan turned onto Golden Byway, then took the exit for Skyview Road. He passed two subdivisions—one filled with efficient small homes that had been there since World War II and another that was in the process of being built, filled with two-story oversized houses and three-car garages. It was as if Crooked Valley Past and Crooked Valley Future had sidled up together. He wasn't sure he liked either world, maybe because he still had a fondness for the street where he grew up, an area filled with low-slung ranch-style homes and expansive yards that hadn't changed too much.

Some would say that was because Raylan didn't like change. He'd never been much of a risk-taker, preferring the worn path to the road less taken. For years, he'd thought that was what he wanted, but lately, he'd been feeling this…restlessness to be more, to do something different. What that something was, he had no idea and didn't plan on finding out. The safe, predictable path had served him well all his life. It's where he should stay.

Another two miles down Skyview Road, standing alone and with an overgrown yard, was the Harrington house. No, not a house, more like a mansion. Although the disappearance of Richard Harrington had been a dinner-table topic for years when Raylan was younger, he'd forgotten many of the small details. He'd skimmed the case file last night before he went home, getting reacquainted with the minutiae, including the fact that the house topped out at 7,200 square feet, with seven bedrooms and five bathrooms. What single Richard Harrington had ever needed with seven bedrooms in one house, as well as a guesthouse and five-car garage, Raylan had no idea.

He saw a white CR-V sitting in the driveway. The car had New York plates and a light coating of road dirt marring a clearly recent run through the car wash. Raylan parked beside Mia's car, then got out of his and picked his way past the weedy driveway to the house. The front door had a heavy board nailed across it, topped with a big red no-trespassing sign, as if the other signs scattered around the property saying the same thing weren't enough. At least Mia hadn't broken into the house. The teenaged Mia he'd dated had been daring and wild, the kind of girl who picked the lock at the town pool on a hot August night and convinced Raylan to go for a midnight swim. The kind of girl who didn't just tempt him to stray from the predictable path—she led him there with a smile and a dare.

Maybe helping her was a big mistake, another deviation from the predictability he loved so much. He told himself that if it brought closure to this town then all of this would be worth the risks he was taking. Or so he hoped.

He skirted the big home and saw her familiar figure heading toward the carriage house, which was located down a second gravel driveway that led to the back of the property. She was still breathtakingly, heart-stoppingly stunning.

Who was he kidding? He was here because she'd hooked him all over again with those big green eyes and that irresistible smile. He was here because there was a part of him that never really closed the door on Mia.

She turned at the sound of his shoes on the gravel. Her eyes widened with surprise and, maybe, a little joy at seeing him. "You came."

He grinned and tried to tame the hope rising in his gut. "Figured I'd try to keep you from breaking the law."

"That was only one time. And we didn't even get caught."

"*Almost* didn't get caught. Not the same thing." An intrepid Crooked Valley police officer had heard noises at the town pool and come over to investigate, just as Mia and Raylan scaled the back fence and took off for the woods. "But now you've grown up to become a law-abiding citizen, right?"

"More or less." She waved at the property. "This might be considered trespassing."

Raylan shook his head. "You're covered. The city took the property to pay for back taxes but hasn't auctioned it off yet. So technically, you're on city-owned land."

"You had to take all the fun and danger out of it, didn't you, Raylan?" She grinned at him, then shivered in her coat. "It's getting colder, and I'd really like to make it through this section of the property before the end of the day. After the sun goes down, it'll be brutally cold."

"This section?" he asked. "Are you doing a grid search?"

She nodded. "That's the best way to do it so you don't retrace your steps or miss anything."

He was impressed with her organization and plan. He'd seen too many armchair "detectives" who went off with abandon, ignoring rules and respect. Mia, however, was going about the whole thing professionally. "The cops searched this property back when Harrington disappeared. I'm pretty sure you're not going to find anything."

She shrugged. "I've found clues where no one else thought to look. I'm sure I can do that in this case, too."

"Maybe so." He had googled Mia late last night and been surprised to see that she hosted what looked like a very successful crime show on YouTube. In several series of short videos, she covered cold cases, updating the viewers every couple of days. She'd taken what had worked so well in the podcast world and turned it into a DIY video show that was exceptionally professional and had several hundred thousand followers. He didn't know much about YouTube, but he was sure a following that large meant Mia had a decent income from her show. More than that, he could see her passion for the cases she worked on, the women she wanted so badly to help find and the murderers she wanted to bring to justice. Nearly all of the cases she focused on had been women who'd disappeared after their partners had abused them. "I saw that you solved some pretty tough cold cases on your show. Very impressive."

"You did an internet search on me?" Her grin widened. "And here I thought all I did was annoy you."

He didn't answer because anything he said would be construed as him caring about her life since they'd been together. And he didn't. Well, he mostly didn't care. Uh-huh. That was why he'd been up in the wee hours watching her series. "I see you've sectioned off the grids already?"

"I have." She turned and pointed at a pattern of sticks with pink-painted ends. She had placed the sticks throughout the yard and then run pink tape between them, forming large squares that were at least thirty yards on each side. "We're in section one today, which goes from the corner of the carriage house there, to the edge of the well there. I'm hoping to search the whole carriage house today and do a ground probe to see if anything's buried beside or behind it. If it's light enough when we make our way to the well, we'll take a peek in there, too."

Her plan made sense and had the markings of a seasoned investigator. Once again, Raylan was impressed. "Why are we starting with the carriage house? I don't remember there being anything particular about that in the police report."

"Because there's a rumor that Richard hid his money on the property, and while it could be in the house, I figured the police have been through that with a fine-tooth comb. Anything they might have missed would be in one of these outbuildings."

"A rumor?" Raylan arched an eyebrow. "From your grandfather's memory, maybe?"

"Can we investigate before we interrogate?" She parked a fist on her hip and glared at him. "I want to conduct this search by thinking like someone other than the police. They would very likely have been more interested in the main house, where Richard spent his daily life, than in the outbuildings."

Mia's instincts were right. The case file had an exhaustive inventory of the contents of the manor, but only a cursory overview of the garage, carriage house and landscaper's shed. They'd done a brief sweep of the well but never climbed inside it. Probably because for several years, the police assumed Harrington was off living the high life in Mexico or the Caribbean. As more time ticked by without any trace of Harrington—or the money—Raylan's father had begun to put together a case for murder. Without a body or any concrete evidence to link Louis Beaumont, however, the case was too flimsy for the grand jury to agree to indict.

Either way, it meant there was a possibility that

crucial evidence had been missed. To the Crooked Valley Police Department, this case was cold and dead. Raylan had called the chief last night and told him there was renewed interest in the case. "Chances are the guy is dead and buried in some foreign country," Chief Cardiff had said. "Go ahead and look if you want, but I doubt there's anything left to find after three decades."

Spending one day on the Harrington property wasn't going to upset Raylan's schedule too much. And if it satisfied Mia's curiosity, or brought some answers that both of them needed, so much the better.

"All right. Let's get to work." He shrugged out of his suit jacket and hung it over the decorative wrought-iron fence in front of the carriage house. Then he uncuffed his shirtsleeves and rolled them up.

"You're really going to help me?"

"I may not be rooting for the same outcome as you, but, yes, I want to get to the bottom of this mystery, too." And, if he was honest with himself, there was a part of Raylan Westfield who was still attracted to and very intrigued by the complex Mia Beaumont, and if searching an old building was a way to spend more time with her, that was fine with him.

The years had not been kind to the once-elegant converted carriage house. Weeds had grown up and over the brick facade, wedging their way into every crack and crevice. Many of the bricks were crumbling or broken, and the boards over the windows were chafed at the edges. The roof had been ripped apart by the weather—maybe that harsh winter they'd just had in Crooked Valley, as some shingles had been torn off altogether, while others had been ripped in two. The marble stairs were tinged green with mold or plant life. Mia wasn't sure which.

She strapped her headlamp onto her head and flicked the switch, then dug in her pocket for a second one and handed it to Raylan. He gave her a dubious look. "It's going to be dark in there. You don't want to trip and rip that fancy suit."

"Clearly, I'm not dressed to go skulking around in boarded-up buildings."

Was he complaining or already trying to leave? "You don't have to be here, Raylan."

"Yes, Mia. I do." There was something serious in Raylan's face, something he wasn't talking about. Once upon a time, she would have cared what that something was, but those days were long in the past. So she brushed off her moment of sentimentality and refocused on why she was here.

"Then I recommend the headlamp." Mia pulled open the door and ducked inside the carriage house. Raylan's light switched on behind her, and the twin headlamp beams illuminated the dark interior. They left the front door open, but the porch was shaded, so it only added a little extra light.

From what she could see, the building had been

used as a guest room/storage space. A pile of boxes sat decaying against one wall. A bed and two chairs were covered with a thick layer of dust. Mice had nibbled at the bedding and mattress, leaving a trail of fluff across the floor. There was a small sitting area, and a kitchenette to one side. All in all, maybe nine hundred square feet of living space, just enough to make a guest comfortable, although it looked like no one had been in here for decades. Mia wasn't surprised. Richard Harrington hadn't had any children or a wife, and if he'd had any other living relatives—and she hadn't found anyone—they wouldn't be able to claim the property until he was declared legally dead. So far, no one had done that.

So the property sat unclaimed, rotting away, until the city of Crooked Valley had finally taken possession. Clearly, the city hadn't done anything about the property yet. Maybe they were waiting for a developer to show some interest. It was a beautiful piece of land—five gorgeous acres filled with trees and lush greenery that backed up to a pond—and would surely sell quickly at auction.

Which was why Mia needed to get what answers she could, before someone bought the Harrington house and tore down the old structures. There could be secrets hidden in these walls or tucked away at the back of a drawer.

"Wow." Raylan's beam bounced over the tented furniture. "This place has really fallen apart."

"It's sad. I bet it was beautiful at one time. Even this little guest cottage is fancier than my apartment in New York." She turned a slow circle. "And about three times larger."

Raylan chuckled. "I don't know how you live in that crowded city after growing up out here, with all the open space and nature."

She started working her way around the room, lifting small pieces of furniture to look underneath, opening drawers and cabinet doors. "There are days when it's hard, I'll admit. I love being outside, but I also love being busy, and New York is perfect for people who don't like to sit still."

"And that's definitely you." He crossed to the bed and shone his headlamp underneath the queen bed-frame. Something skittered away and darted into the corner, but Raylan barely flinched. "You got in trouble so many times in school for not sitting still."

She grinned. Raylan was right about that. Mia remembered being bored stiff when she was stuck in a classroom, desperate to go outside and do something active. "I wasn't the only one getting in trouble. I seem to remember you getting detention for reading in math class."

"I still think that was wrong. I was reading in school. Nothing the matter with that."

She laughed as they had a debate she remembered well from their younger years. Mia's trouble had always come from acting up, whereas Raylan's stemmed from being too studious. "Still trying to fight your punishment?"

"Argue till the end. I have to. I'm a lawyer." He moved to the closet and opened the door. "What exactly are we looking for here?"

"Whatever looks like a clue. I don't really know." She shone her flashlight on the stack of boxes. They seemed to be the standard storage items—Christmas decorations, winter clothes, ski gear. Unless the labels were a lie, she doubted there was anything worth finding in there.

"I think we should look in them, anyway," Raylan said, reading her mind. "Let me take down these drapes so we have some more light." He yanked at the heavy velvet curtains. They tore in his hands and tumbled to the floor. Then he jerked up one of the windows and used a heavy lamp to knock the plywood boards off and onto the lawn. Sunlight flooded into the room, transforming the space and revealing all the dust and despair.

"Thanks."

"I can be useful." His blue eyes sparkled. The corners of his eyes still crinkled in that way that made it seem like his entire face was laughing. It was endearing and handsome all at the same time, and it made her remember a simpler, happier time between them.

There was a moment happening here, a moment that Mia didn't want to acknowledge. The old attraction to Raylan brewed inside her, and she fought against allowing that feeling any room in her heart.

Falling for Raylan again was a complication she didn't need. She was going back to New York after this was over and leaving Raylan Westfield in her past, where he belonged.

"Let's, uh, get into those boxes before it gets too late," she said. "There's a lot of ground to cover before the end of the day."

"Sounds like a plan."

For a couple of hours, they worked their way through the boxes, digging their way past stored Christmas lights and ski boots. Raylan talked about cases he'd prosecuted over the years, and Mia talked about some of the cases she'd covered on her show. Time passed quickly, and when they reached the final box, Mia was a little disappointed. She'd enjoyed working so closely with Raylan, more than she'd like to admit.

"Well, that's it." She got to her feet and wiped the worst of the dust off her pants. "We can move on to searching the grounds. I've got some pointed sticks we can use to penetrate any section that looks suspicious."

Raylan stacked the boxes into a reasonably neat pile. It wasn't something he needed to do—the man who used the things in those boxes was long gone—but it was a typical Raylan move. She had to admit she found it sweet. "Raylan the Responsible strikes again." She shot him a grin.

He rolled his eyes at the use of the high-school nickname. "I'm just trying to be nice."

"Richard is the only one who would care about

what happens to his Christmas decorations, and I'm pretty positive he's never going to decorate again."

"True. But it's the right thing to do."

Mia's heart softened even more toward Raylan. He had always been thoughtful and seemed even more so as an adult. Thoughtfulness was a trait that it seemed too few people had. Maybe living in the city had made her jaded and mistrustful, or maybe she was just feeling a little sentimental.

Or maybe Raylan Westfield had grown up to be a really nice guy.

She shrugged off those thoughts. She had one chance to uncover any mysteries the Harrington mansion might hold, and she wasn't going to waste that with romantic thoughts that had nowhere to go but down a road full of mistakes. She paced the room, making sure they'd checked every nook and cranny. "Did you finish going through the closet?"

"There was a bunch of clothes piled up on the floor in there, beside a bunch of shoes and a bin full of dumbbells. Looks like someone changed their minds about getting in shape."

"But this is a guesthouse. Why would the closet be full of clothes and shoes? Either there was a long-term guest here—and nothing in the police file mentions anyone staying here at the time Richard disappeared—or he was using this for clothing storage, which doesn't make sense because the house has seven bedrooms and seven closets at minimum. In fact, why is he storing anything at all in here when the house had plenty of room?"

"You're right. That is odd. And it's a bit of a walk from the main house if you want your winter boots."

Their eyes met, and they both nodded at the same time, then crossed to the closet without a word. Mia sifted through the pile. "These are dresses and women's sweaters. There's no mention of a woman in the Harrington file."

"Maybe he had a girlfriend? Or was renting this space?"

"I don't know, but it seems odd that no one uncovered that detail." Raylan and Mia hoisted the clothes and shoes out of the closet and laid them on the floor, then switched on their headlamps and stepped inside the spacious walk-in. "I don't see anything else in here."

"You said you thought he hid the money in his house. Maybe he hid it in the guesthouse. He could have a safe or something hidden in the wall."

"Good idea." Mia began rapping on the walls while Raylan did the same. They worked their way from the front corners to the middle, while also going up and down, from chest-high to the floor. Everything sounded solid and normal.

Until Mia rapped the section of wall to the left of the back corner. Instead of the normal *thump-thump*, she heard a hollow thud, as if something had been stuffed into the wall. She rocked back on her heels and looked over at Raylan. "Did you hear that?"

"It sounds like there's something in there."

Mia's heart began to race. This could be the answer. This could be everything. "Let's open it up."

Chapter Three

Raylan ducked outside to grab a tire iron from the trunk of his car, admittedly feeling a little excited, like he had when he was a kid and had gone on exploration trips with his father. Really, the trips had been nothing more than traipsing through the woods early in the morning, but his father had made every trip seem like an adventure, as if there could be anything—an ancient city, a buried treasure, a fragile fawn—around the corner. His love of exploring, questioning and uncovering was what had made him follow in his father's footsteps and enter the law. Today, however, was the first time he'd ever been truly hands-on with a case. And to tell the truth, it was pretty exciting.

While he was gone, Mia had set up a video camera on a tripod and a stand lamp in the opposite corner of the closet. The space was illuminated well and made his job of removing the drywall much easier.

The old walls began to crumble as he poked a hole near a stud and then began peeling them back. Nails screeched in protest at being pulled out of timbers. The first chunk came off and broke as it hit the carpeted floor.

"Do you see anything?" Mia asked.

Raylan fished his flashlight out of his back pocket as Mia came closer with the camera and lamp. They shone their lights into the space and saw...

Nothing. Just a pair of two-by-fours and a thick white electrical line running toward the outlet outside the closet. "Sorry, Mia."

He stepped back. Mia put a hand on his shoulder. "Wait. Don't move. Shine your light a little more down and to the right. Do you see that?"

Even with both their flashlights, headlamps and the stand lamp, the light was swallowed by the darkness deep in the walls. He took a step closer, angling his flashlight as he did. A flash of something shimmered in the far recesses of the wall. "It looks like some plastic."

"Open the rest of the closet. We need to get farther into that wall."

He started to pull off more drywall, working his way down the interior wall of the closet. Whatever was behind the wall was stuffed into the space to the right of the closet, toward the corner of the room. The walls here, designed to support what looked like a load-bearing wall and the closet framing, were a nest of timbers that obscured most of the view. Raylan concentrated on taking out the far closet wall and all of the drywall in front of whatever they had seen.

It didn't take long before the piece of plastic began to take shape. A very distinctive, large shape that looked a lot like…

Like a body that had been tipped forward and pushed deep into the recesses of the wall.

"Wow. A body!" Mia scooted past Raylan to shine her light and camera on the hunched figure. "In our search today," she said as she videotaped, "we uncovered a body. The plastic is too thick to see if it's a man or a woman. Since it's been thirty years since anyone has been in this house, chances are we're looking at a skeleton, which means it'll be a while before we have any answers. Let me just…" She took a pocketknife out of her pocket.

Raylan grabbed her wrist. "This is now a crime scene, Mia. We can't disturb it any more than we already have. It's time to call in the police."

He could see the frustration in her face at being stopped from opening the plastic and seeing who was wrapped inside. "I need answers, Raylan."

"And you'll have them." He pulled his cell phone out of his pocket. "*After* the Crooked Valley Police Department processes the scene."

She stood there a moment longer, clearly wanting to argue the point. "Fine." Mia grabbed her tripod and stormed out of the closet.

A few minutes later, several members of the Crooked Valley Police Department were on the scene.

Crooked Valley was growing every year but hadn't reached the level of needing a full-time forensics department. After the string of arsons the town had gone through a few months ago, they'd hired a single forensic specialist, a young woman who wasn't much for small talk but was exceptionally good at her job.

Raylan got out of the way while Farrah Patel, the forensics specialist, did her job, analyzing, bagging and tagging. The coroner had done his preliminary exam of the body, which wasn't much because the space was too small to fit the plump man. After the pictures and search of the space were completed, a pair of officers carried the plastic bundle out of the closet and set it on a gurney.

The plastic tarp had been wrapped around the body several times and tied with a thick rope. It was clear, just from the way the tarp was shaped, that whoever this once was had become a skeleton, as Mia had said earlier.

Mia came up beside Raylan. He caught the light floral scent of her perfume, and for a second, it was a dozen years ago and they were standing outside the community center, making the hard decision to break up and go their separate ways.

He shook his head. He was standing at a crime scene. That was not the time to be thinking about a woman he used to date. A woman, he reminded himself, who was on the opposing side of this crime.

Farrah came up to Raylan, snapping off her latex gloves as she did. "I won't know much until the coro-

ner does the autopsy, but it looks like we have someone who's been deceased a very long time, which
will probably make it more difficult to determine
cause of death."

"Is it Richard Harrington?" Mia leaned a little
closer, as if trying to read Farrah's notes.

Farrah's gaze narrowed. "Are you with the police
department?"

"No, I'm—"

"She's a friend," Raylan interrupted, then wondered why he had done that. Defining Mia as his
friend—or his anything, for that matter—was as far
from the truth as he could get. They were nothing at
this stage in their lives. Just two people who used to
date when they were kids. "She's okay, Farrah. You
can talk in front of her."

Farrah assessed Mia. "You're with the DA's office,
so if you say she's okay, I'll trust your word, but I'm
only going to discuss broad strokes in front of a ci-
vilian. Detective Morales is heading to the morgue to
watch the autopsy. I'm going back to my office and
will start processing what evidence we have. We'll
be checking the tarp for fingerprints and combing
through the crime scene in more depth today. I doubt
there's anything else in those walls, but we won't
know for sure until we open them up more fully."

Raylan thanked Farrah. Mia started moving toward her, but Raylan stopped her. "If you want my
cooperation, Mia, you can't go questioning my in-

vestigators, especially when they made it clear they don't want to share sensitive information with you."

"I hate to break this to you, Raylan, but that is exactly how investigations work." Annoyance flashed in her features. "People ask questions."

"Law enforcement asks questions. Media waits for what answers we give them."

She arched an eyebrow. "Come on, Raylan. You know me. You know why I want to—no, need to—solve this case right now."

"Whether you like it or not, whether your grandfather is a suspect or not, you are still a member of the media, Mia. That means I can't and won't tell you everything. This is an ongoing investigation and not something I want splashed all over YouTube." Why was he holding such a hard line with her? He knew Mia and knew she could be trusted. At the same time, he found himself using his job to insert some mental and emotional distance between them.

"And yet you overlooked that fact when you came scavenger hunting with me today."

He shook his head. "That was a mistake."

"A mistake that found the body of Richard Harrington."

"That *possibly* found his body," he reminded her. "It could be someone else."

"That man disappeared thirty years ago from this exact address, maybe on purpose. I don't think there are a whole lot of other bodies that are going to turn up in the walls." Mia let out a little chuckle. "Raylan, the coincidence is too easy."

She had a point, but Raylan was a man of facts, and until he had more of those, he wasn't going to make a lot of assumptions. "Either way, it can't be suicide. There's no way someone wrapped themselves in plastic and crammed their own body into the closet wall of the carriage house."

"Obviously someone did that to him."

"Someone who had a lot to gain, especially financially. Maybe his business partner?" The words were out of Raylan's mouth before he could stop them, his mental thought process erupting in front of the last person who wanted to hear that accusation.

Mia's face crumpled at the implication that her grandfather was involved. A flash of emotion showed in her eyes, but she shook it off and took a step back. "I'm done here today. Turns out law enforcement is in the way, anyhow." She gave him a pointed look that lumped him in with the Crooked Valley Police Department, then packed up her gear and left.

Raylan told himself he was glad. Mia was a disruption he didn't need. Not today. Not on any day.

Chapter Four

Mia sat in her grandfather's driveway for a long time, debating how much to tell him. Her grandfather was old, fragile, just getting over chemotherapy, and she didn't want to upset him unnecessarily. However, if that body did turn out to be Richard's, there was a very real chance her grandfather could get arrested.

He was nearly eighty years old. Arresting a man at that age was inhumane. Mia worried that involving Raylan would turn out to be a colossal mistake, one that could cost her grandfather everything he held dear.

She couldn't let Grandpa Louis be unprepared for whatever might be coming and how that might impact his life. The discovery of the body at the Harrington house would undoubtedly be on the news. If it wasn't already a breaking alert, it would be on the next newscast. A handful of reporters had heard the call for the detectives on the police scanner and shown up right after the coroner did. Raylan and the police chief had refused to answer any questions, promising an update for the media sometime in the future, but Mia knew that would only delay the inevitable news reports. She was in the same industry and couldn't begrudge the journalists who were just doing their jobs.

While the reporters were busy badgering Raylan, Mia managed to sneak out undetected and without having to give an interview or explain her presence amid all the police officers. She had no doubt, though, that some savvy journalist would track down the car with out-of-state plates and put the pieces together.

Because that was what Mia would do. When she'd solved the case of the missing teenager in Queens, she'd done much the same thing. In the background of one of the police photos there'd been a late model sedan idling on the side of the road, the driver looking like he was waiting on someone. The car seemed unusual for the area, which was relatively well-to-do. Mia had scoured the photo archives of the reporters who had been there until she came across another photo of the car, this one with a full license plate. She'd tracked the plate to a registered sex offender living in New Jersey. She'd partnered with the local police, giving them the information that she had, which had been enough for a search warrant. A full day of searching later, they'd found the body of the missing girl buried in the man's backyard, hidden under a recently built planter. It wasn't the happy ending Mia had hoped for, but it had brought answers and closure to a grieving family.

Lord, please make this case work out for my grandfather. Let me prove his innocence.

It was a prayer she'd whispered many times over the last few weeks. The problem was how to do that. She couldn't prove that Grandpa was home sick that day—the only person who could vouch for his illness was her grandmother, who had passed away a few years ago. They had a statement from Grandma, but Mia was sure a wife vouching for a husband who was a murder suspect didn't carry a lot of weight. Besides, it was surely feasible to the cops that Grandpa could have left long enough to commit a murder, while Grandma thought he was still at home. That was what Mia would have thought, if she didn't know her grandfather so well and know he would never hurt, much less kill, anyone.

Which meant Mia needed to prove her grandfather wasn't at the bank that day withdrawing the money, or somewhere murdering Richard. Proving someone *wasn't* where they were purported to be was an almost impossible task. It was either that or prove someone else had been there.

Mia left Grandpa's and went back through town until she reached the Harrington property again. She headed down the long driveway of Richard's house, passing a half-dozen police cars and several unmarked vehicles as well as the coroner's van and the forensic unit van. As she emerged from the tree line, she saw a flicker of something dark dash between the stately oaks that lined the driveway.

Maybe a deer. She slowed to make the turn onto Skyview Road, and out of the corner of her left eye, she saw the unmistakable silhouette of a man dressed in all black, his face obscured by an oversized sweat-shirt hood. Watching her. A chill slithered down her spine. Then, just as quickly as she saw him, he disappeared, so neatly and easily she half believed he'd been a mirage.

By the time she pulled into Grandpa Louis's drive-way, she had convinced herself that the man had been a reporter, sneaking through the woods, hoping to see or overhear something he could use to break the case wide open. She may not have been able to see the man clearly, but she'd seen enough to know it was impossible that he was a millionaire who'd disappeared thirty years ago and would now be in his mid-seventies.

Mia shrugged it off as she climbed out of the car and went up the porch stairs. She took a deep breath and then pulled open the door, expecting to find the same situation as the day before. Instead, her grand-father was sitting at the kitchen table going through the stack of newspaper articles Mia had printed from the archives. He was taking notes on a legal pad and looked up when Mia entered. "Hello, granddaughter." A smile crossed his face. "I decided it's time I help you with this investigation. Hoping one of these articles you found might trigger a memory. I'm writing down everything that comes to mind."

It warmed Mia's heart to see her grandfather excited and invested, even if the stakes were so terrifyingly high. That meant her coming here had been a good thing for him. "That's great, Grandpa. It's so nice to see you up and about."

"How did the search go today?"

Grandpa skimmed an article that theorized Richard was living in a foreign country. There hadn't been much in the media three decades ago. Once the police said they assumed Richard had left the United States, the reporters pretty much dropped the story. Richard had become the reclusive millionaire who was living the high life on other people's money. There'd been a flurry of articles when Frank Westfield tried to indict Grandpa Louis, but when the grand jury voted against indictment, the media went back to the original theory of Richard sitting on a beach somewhere. All of which meant there was little, if any, useful information about Richard in the newspapers.

Because the disappearance had happened so long ago, most of the newspapers didn't even have the material in online archives, which had made for tedious work finding the articles that did exist. When she was in New York, she'd done what she could through the internet, searching some of the major metropolitan papers in Colorado. Now that she was in town, she hoped to visit some of the smaller local publications to see if they had anything in their "morgue" of past clippings. It was a lot of footwork, but worth it if she found something.

"I need to talk to you about the search. We found something." Mia pulled out one of the chairs and sat down across from her grandfather. "A body."

Grandpa Louis stilled. For a long moment, he stared down at the paper, as if dreading what she was about to say. "Is it Richard?"

"We don't know yet. The body was wrapped in a tarp. It's been there for quite some time, and there wasn't enough…well, it's going to take dental records to figure out who it is."

Her grandfather raised his gaze to hers. His eyes were filled with a mix of emotions—worry, sadness, hope. "So it's possible it's not Richard."

"Possible. But unlikely it's not him. Who else would be there?" Richard had been the only one living in the mansion. He'd had a groundskeeper and a maid who came in every day to take care of the massive house, but neither one of them was missing. She'd read the police interviews with Richard's staff, and neither of them had seen or noticed anything—or anyone—suspicious in the days leading up to his disappearance.

"Don't worry." Grandpa covered her hand with his own. "We don't know what we don't know. The good news is that we are one step closer to solving this mystery."

"But if it turns out to be Richard…" She couldn't

bring herself to say the words, to pop that bubble of hope on her grandfather's face.

"I know what could happen, but I've put my faith in God that this will turn out exactly as it's meant to."

"Even if that means you're arrested for a crime you didn't commit?"

"If I am, that means God is using me for some other purpose." Grandpa gave Mia's hand a squeeze. "I've lived a great life, Mia. I'm okay with whatever happens."

Mia was not okay with the idea of her grandfather going to jail. All the excitement she'd felt when they found the body had disappeared. If it turned out to be Richard…

"For now," Grandpa went on, interrupting her thoughts, "we have all this information to go through. Why don't you get the file you put together and we'll see if two brains are better than one."

"Sounds like a plan, Grandpa." Not to mention, the *only* plan she had right now.

Raylan spent most of his Saturday morning researching Richard Harrington. He'd gone through the files his father had kept and also done a Google search of any newspaper articles that might have been digitized for the archives, but there wasn't much. The police report was pretty lean. The disappearance of a single man who lived alone hadn't left much evidence or many witnesses for the cops to work with, so Raylan wasn't surprised. It was what he *didn't* see that surprised him—the evidence that Louis Beaumont was involved. His father had been a great prosecutor, but not the most organized person, so it was possible that file was somewhere else in the office. Raylan made a note to check with Susan.

Raylan had already had a conversation with Hugh Levine, his boss and the district attorney, early this morning. Like Raylan, Hugh worked weekends and late nights—he was a man who was fully dedicated to his job. It was too early to speculate a prosecutorial course of action, but the unspoken message was clear—if the body was Harrington's, the first person they were questioning was Louis Beaumont. An envious, angry or greedy business partner was the most logical choice for a main suspect.

The coroner called a little after one that afternoon. "This is an interesting one," Harry Jenson said when Raylan picked up. Harry had been the Crooked Valley coroner for almost ten years and had always done an excellent job. He was well-known for his attention to detail and puzzle-solving whenever he was given a difficult case.

"Interesting good or interesting bad?"

"Just plain interesting." Harry paused a beat, something he often did just to draw out the drama. He told everyone that he loved his job and loved being able to surprise people with the answers he found. "First off, the body you found is not Richard Harrington's."

Raylan sat back in his desk chair. That did indeed make this case interesting and changed every assumption he'd just had. "Are you sure?"

"The remains are skeletal, but there's no doubt this is the body of a woman. I won't get into all the technicalities of bone growth and dental eruptions, but I estimate that she was maybe twenty-three, at most twenty-seven. No signs of ever having had children. Short, about five foot two, and with a small build. Dental records will give us more information. There was no ID or anything else with the body, so I don't know who she is yet."

"I think I do." Raylan opened the file on his desk and flipped a few pages. "Danielle Sondheim, the assistant to Richard and Louis. They have a photocopy of her DMV information here and what it says fits that height and weight. The police report says she moved away a couple weeks before Richard's disappearance, but it looks like they never interviewed her. There's just a couple notes saying they tried to find out where she moved to, and the trail ran cold."

"Well, I think it's about time they figure out where she was supposed to have gone and why she didn't get there. Because someone is missing this girl and deserves some answers."

But if someone was missing Danielle, they would have notified the Crooked Valley police. There was no indication of a missing person report being filed on Richard's assistant. That seemed odd to Raylan. Maybe people had been looking for her in the wrong location, because it looked like she'd never left Crooked Valley after all. "Any indications of the cause of death?"

"Bullet to the skull." Harry sighed. "At least whatever happened to her was quick."

"Thank God for that." Murder of any kind was a senseless tragedy, but at least this woman hadn't spent hours bleeding out, or worse, years hooked up to machines. Raylan thanked Harry, then hung up with one hand while he scribbled notes on the legal pad with his other. He flipped through the file again, looking for more information on Danielle, but there wasn't much, maybe because she'd never been called as a witness. She had grown up in foster care ever since she was a baby, had no other siblings, but did have a husband, Paul, who was surely wondering where she was. Unless he was her killer, which could very well be the case. Maybe Harrington's assistant got greedy and tried to extort money from her boss, which had led to Harrington firing that fatal bullet? If so, why hadn't her husband reported her missing? Or maybe she was having an affair with him and when Paul found out, he killed her? There were a thousand possibilities for motive, but after so much time passing, a lot of the truth was undoubtedly lost forever.

Raylan called the lead detective, Joe Morales, and exchanged the information he had with the officer. Morales had already talked to Harry and had much the same idea as Raylan—if Danielle's husband was still out there, then his failure to report his wife's disappearance looked pretty incriminating.

But none of that solved the mystery of where Richard Harrington might be. Or what his disappearance had to do with Danielle's murder. What had seemed like a simple case was now ten times more complex.

He heard a knock on his door and looked up to see Mia standing in the doorway. Her dark blond hair fell to her shoulders in loose curls that offset her heart-shaped face and deep green eyes. She'd worn jeans and an oversized white sweater today, along with a pair of brown leather boots. She looked gorgeous and comfortable all at the same time, and for a second, he wondered what might have been if they'd never broken up. "What are you doing here?"

"I could ask the same of you. It's Saturday." Mia entered the room and perched on the arm of the visitor chair. "Most people take time off on the weekends."

"Says the pot to the kettle." He grinned and she smiled back. There were times when he forgot they were at opposite ends of this case. Forgot that they'd once been something and then broken up. Forgot that she was the last girl in the world he should fall for because they wanted different things out of life.

"Well, they have the crime scene roped off now, which means pretty much the entire Harrington estate is off-limits to everyone, especially media, so I had to suspend my search." Mia frowned. "That throws a wrench into my plans."

He could hear the hint in her voice, the question she didn't ask. "I can't let you onto a crime scene, Mia. You could contaminate evidence, and I could lose my job."

"I know. I was hoping you'd maybe want to exchange notes." She gave him a hopeful smile. "Two heads are better than one, or so they say."

The way her entire face lit up when she smiled socked him in the gut. Mia was a beautiful woman all the time, but her smile made her radiant, dazzling, irresistible. He steeled his spine and reminded himself that she was here to clear the name of the same man Raylan was possibly going to indict. "You want to know what the prosecutor has in his files? When one of the suspects is your grandfather?"

"Well, when you put it that way…" Her eyes danced with amusement, with the familiar tease that he remembered so very well. "Yeah, I do."

"Mia, I can't do that."

She slid over the arm of the chair and dropped into the seat, then leaned forward and rested her elbows on his desk. "I don't want to ruin whatever case you might build out of this. We both want answers, though, and I still think that we can solve this together."

"What makes you think we can do what my father and the police department couldn't?"

"We have more invested." A shadow dropped over her features. "My grandfather is getting older and frailer, and I worry that I won't solve this before he…" She glanced away for a second, then gathered her emotions and turned back. "Either way, I'm asking you, Raylan, as a friend, to work with me on this. No matter what the outcome is, my grandfather needs and deserves those answers."

The entreaty in her eyes tugged at his heartstrings, made him want to throw all the rules out the window. But now that the investigation had been reopened and there was another body involved, Raylan knew he shouldn't allow Mia to get anywhere near the evidence. He couldn't just open his files and let her have a look.

She had a point about her emotional investment, however. Her love and protectiveness of her grandfather was clear, and he could understand why she and Louis would want this case put to rest, just as he wanted to do the same for a father who couldn't remember the past. Raylan also knew Mia was a stubborn, dogged woman who would work tirelessly until she achieved whatever goal she set her mind to. She could be a good ally in this mystery, if only because of her smarts and determination.

Yeah, that was why he wanted to work with her. Not because seeing her stirred something in his heart or because defining them as friends caused a little ache inside his chest. Maybe it was that ache or maybe it was her asking so nicely, but Raylan decided it couldn't hurt to get her take on the evidence.

"How about a compromise? I can't let you into my files or onto the crime scene, but I can tell you what the coroner told me. The body is a woman's. We think it's Richard and Louis's assistant, Danielle." Raylan caught her up on the other information Harry had given him, sticking to just the facts, not any interpretations he had or any indication of where he was leaning legally.

"Wow. That's not what I was expecting to hear. I'm going to have to dig into Danielle's past now. She's barely a footnote in the case."

"I know. I don't have much on her, either. She was supposed to have moved out of town weeks before Richard disappeared."

"This just gets more and more curious as time goes on. Do you think maybe Richard killed Danielle before he went missing?"

Raylan leaned back and ran a hand through his hair. "I don't know. All I know for sure is that we need more information than we have."

"Then I better get to work and start going through some archives." She got to her feet, as if she was about to leave.

Before she could, Raylan said, "If you want more of my mental notes, you're going to have to buy me lunch."

What was that? Had he just asked her on a date? No, no. It was two colleagues sharing notes over some food, nothing more. The anticipation of her answer stirring in his gut called him a liar.

"Deal." She wagged a finger at him, amusement

sparkling in her eyes. "But only because you mentioned food."

Raylan chuckled as he slipped on his jacket and followed her to the door. "That was one thing we had in common. We both loved a good meal."

"Especially if it involved burgers and fries."

"Then how about taking a stroll down memory lane and having lunch at Cappy's Diner?" Raylan shut the door behind them and locked his office. "Uh, food memories, not dating memories."

"Just to be clear," she said.

"Of course." They were just friends, after all. Or something like that.

As they stepped out into the bright sunshine and headed down the sidewalk toward Cappy's, he realized the moment could have been a carbon copy from when they were dating. They'd dated for a year, frequenting the diner at least once a week, not just because it was where they had their first date but because the food was amazing. Back then, they'd been high-school students working part-time, minimum-wage jobs, so they usually ended up splitting whatever they ordered. He could remember Mia's laughter and her smile and how happy she'd made him back then.

Until she broke it off and moved away, and the future he'd thought they were going to have disappeared. Rightly so, because they had wanted totally different lives. Mia had wanted to see the world and live without restrictions. Raylan had wanted to stay right here, making a difference in the town he loved so much. He'd dreamed of a wife and kids and a picket-fence life, but that had never come about. Maybe because he worked too much. Or maybe because he'd never forgotten his first love.

As soon as they entered the diner, they were greeted by Cappy Winstead, the owner. The old, wizened man with a smattering of white hair on his head was close to eighty now, but still showed up every day to seat guests and chat with people he knew. "Mia Beaumont, why, as I live and breathe. What brings you back to Crooked Valley?" Cappy drew Mia into a hug. "I've missed my best waitress."

"I've missed you, too, Cappy, and this lovely place." Mia grinned. "I'm just visiting my grandpa for a little while. But if I need some part-time work—"

"There's always a job here for you." Cappy's features softened. "It's good to see you, kid."

"Good to see you, too." Her eyes misted. "You still making the best burgers around?"

"Best burgers in the state of Colorado, you mean? Of course." Cappy peered around Mia. "And would you look at who is with you. Raylan! How have you been?"

"Hey, Cappy, good to see you." Raylan had known Cappy for so long that coming here was a lot like returning home for Christmas. Everything stayed the same in this diner, which was a little time capsule to all his best memories.

The older man clapped Raylan on the back. "About

time you stopped in to say hello. Can't remember the last time you were in here."

"I know. I don't get time to go out for lunch very often. I order a lot of takeout from this diner, though." Standing here beside Mia made Raylan realize that she was one of the reasons he'd avoided coming into the diner. Every inch of the place reminded him of her, from the red-leather barstools to the high-back booths with their mini jukeboxes.

"Of course." He motioned for them to follow him. "Let's get you two situated, and then I'll bring you a couple Dr Peppers and Cappy Special burgers. With extra ketchup."

"I can't believe you remember our order so well." Mia sat in the booth. "We haven't been here in more than a decade."

Cappy waved off her comment. "Some people are harder to forget than others. You two let me know if you need anything else." He hurried over to the soda dispenser and began filling two plastic glasses.

It hadn't escaped Raylan's attention that Cappy had also seated them at the same booth that the two of them had chosen every time they came to the diner when they were younger. It was the back booth, perfect for two teenagers who just wanted to be alone. He met Mia's gaze as he sat down across from her. The tension between them was thick with memories and regrets.

Mia glanced away first, busying herself with the first thing she saw. "Oh, look, he still has the jukeboxes. But they're digital now. Apparently you can control them with an app."

"Even Cappy is entering the twenty-first century." Raylan chuckled. "Should we download the app? Maybe play some Bruno Mars or Katy Perry?" The music of his high-school years and the year he'd dated Mia.

She slowly shook her head. "We're here to work, Raylan. Not pretend we're eighteen again."

Except that was impossible every time he looked at her. Maybe it was being in this booth, surrounded by a dozen scents and sights that reminded him of Mia, but all Raylan could think about was where and why things went wrong between them. "What happened to us, Mia?"

She sighed. "Let's not do this."

Instead of responding, he waited, leaving the silence between them. Hoping she would fill it with answers he already knew but was having trouble remembering.

"We both know this answer. I wasn't ready for anything long-term and all you wanted was to stay in the same place and settle down," she said finally. "We were heading in two different directions and wanted two different lives. You're all small-town, fenced-in yard and kids, and I'm cities and freedom and adventures."

That was true. From the time he'd been old enough to realize what family meant, he'd wanted one of his own. His parents had had a good marriage, full of laughter and great memories, something Raylan had always craved for himself. Although he'd dated several women since he and Mia broke up, none of them had made him feel the way she had. None of them had made him think about forever like she had. "People change, though. Their goals change. Their dreams change."

"Some people do, Raylan. But not all."

That didn't answer Raylan's implied question of whether her heart had changed. He'd sensed a bit of wistfulness in her eyes every time she looked at the mountains or a favorite place from years ago. Maybe Mia wasn't all cities and freedom and adventures anymore. And maybe Raylan was just wishing for the impossible.

"Speaking of ancient history." Mia interrupted his thoughts. "Tell me about the Harrington property. I heard it used to be a gold mine or something? Or is that just a Crooked Valley legend?"

The change of subject placed a clear dividing line between them, one he should pay attention to. The only thing he should be thinking about was the case, because it was the only thing he could do something about. "Actually, the part about the gold is true. There's been gold in Colorado before it was even a state. Back in the late 1850s, a man named George Simpson found gold dust in a creek near Denver, while another man found some nuggets nearby. Once word got out, it set off the Colorado gold rush."

"I thought that was only in California." Mia pulled a notepad out of her bag and began jotting notes.

"That's what lots of people think. Truth is, we had our own here for a while, starting in 1858. Hundreds of people began flocking to Colorado to search for gold. An even bigger discovery of gold chunks in January of 1859 opened the floodgates. The people who came here built houses, which became towns, which became cities like Denver and Aurora."

"Wow. I didn't know that. Probably because I never paid attention in history class."

He chuckled. "Whereas I was glued to everything history. A total nerd."

"I wouldn't call you a nerd, Raylan," she said softly.

He tapped his glasses instead of trying to see what mysteries lay in her deep green eyes. "I fit the stereotype, though."

"You don't look like any nerd I've ever seen. More like a really nice version of Clark Kent." She blushed, then shook her head. "So, uh, Harrington's property was the site for some of this prospecting?"

She thought he looked like a superhero's alter ego? Raylan tucked away that tidbit of information. Maybe things between them weren't as dead as he'd thought.

"Uh, yes." He cleared his throat and refocused on their purpose for being here. "In 1861, Harrington's great-great-great-grandfather Isaiah discovered some gold in the creek that runs along the edge of the property. It was worth just enough for him to buy all five acres, build the original house that was there—Harrington remodeled and expanded it when he made his fortune—and then set up what was essentially a tourist attraction. Isaiah knew that eventually the prospectors would find the majority of the gold buried here, and he wanted to build a business that would last long into the future."

"Smart."

"Very smart." Raylan thanked Cappy as he delivered the sodas and they exchanged some more small talk with the owner of the diner. So much of this moment was déjà vu, and at the same time, it was all new ground for them to cover. They weren't teenagers giggling in the back booth, silly with love and lofty dreams. They were adults trying to bring answers to this town and solve a murder.

"Tell me more about the gold-mining business," Mia said after Cappy left. "I know the gold rush in Colorado probably has nothing to do with Harrington's disappearance, but I think the more facts I am working with about that property and Harrington's ancestors, the better."

"Well, I know a lot of the history, so I have plenty of facts for you." Raylan took a sip of his Dr Pepper. The scent of the burgers cooking on the grill made his stomach rumble. "For a month or two, Isaiah Harrington lived on that piece of property alone, with no neighbors for miles. Then word of what he called the 'River of Gold' began to spread, and people started moving here, hoping to strike it rich for a lot lower cost than the prospectors had to pay if they wanted to go West. There were also a lot of entrepreneurial folks setting up shop in the towns that led to Colorado and California, and a lot of desperate people who paid up to six hundred dollars—half a year's pay—for a set of oxen, a wagon, tools and tents to get them across the country."

"And so few of them probably found any gold at the end of that journey." Mia shook her head. "That's so sad."

Raylan thought of all those hopeful, eager families who had very likely invested their life's savings in a dream that came true for only a few. What a parallel to the people who had lost their money when Harrington disappeared. They'd all dreamed of making enough to retire easy, or quit working, and in an instant, those dreams were gone in the wind, with the man they had trusted. "Those are the people who founded this area. Historians think up to forty thousand people came through Colorado on their quest to find gold. Thousands settled down here, which was why so many towns and cities sprang up in this area. Sadly, in doing so, they displaced many, many Native Americans and used up their precious resources of timber and buffalo."

"What a sad, tragic part of our history. So many people were hurt over something as silly as a piece of land and a shiny rock." She sipped her soda while she made more notes, filling the long yellow pad with information. "What happened with the Harringtons?"

"Isaiah Harrington wasn't lying about the River of Gold, although he was the one who profited from it the most. It was rumored that he discovered a half a million dollars' worth, which would have been like hitting the lottery in today's world."

"Two Cappy Specials?" A waitress, a young girl in her teens who probably went to the same Crooked Valley High that Mia and Raylan had attended, set their plates on the table. The thick burgers were piled high with toppings and several slices of cheese. Gooey, decadent goodness in a fluffy bun.

Mia thanked the waitress. When Raylan went to take a bite, Mia put a hand on his arm. "Can we say grace first?"

Raylan blinked, surprised not just by the touch, but by her request. He'd never known Mia to be much for going to church or abiding by any rules, most of all God's. "Since when do you say grace?"

"Since I realized that God has brought me to some pretty amazing places in my life and also some pretty scary ones. He's had my back in every investigation I've done, and because of that, I've grown my channel into something that actually makes enough money to pay New York City rents." Mia shrugged. "I'm just grateful overall. For a lot of things."

He wondered what those other things were and if there would ever be a day when Mia opened up enough to tell him. "I think that's wonderful, Mia."

They both bowed their heads. Mia's voice was soft and sweet as she prayed over their meal. "Dear

Lord, thank You for this food. For bringing me here to help my grandfather. Please help us to solve this case soon. Amen."

It was a nice moment, an unexpected moment. There were all these new dimensions to this adult Mia Beaumont that surprised and intrigued him. When they'd been younger, he'd been in love with her, but it had been a puppy love, one that was all stars in his eyes and a constant yearning. Twelve years later, the craving to be with her was deeper, circling around knowing what made her tick, what had brought her to this stage of her life and where she wanted to go next.

They both started eating and agreed that the Cappy Special burger was the best burger they'd ever had. Their conversation revolved around how Crooked Valley had changed since Mia went away, the arrest of the arsonist who had threatened the Beaumont family coffee shop and the businesses of several other people and the new highway that was being built just outside town. The conversation flowed as easily as a river between them.

Raylan had trouble concentrating on anything other than Mia's deep green eyes and the magic of her smile. He noticed she had a smudge of ketchup on the side of her lip, and before he could think better of it, Raylan leaned across the table and swiped away the smudge with his finger. A look of surprise flitted across her face at his touch.

"You had a little ketchup there." He sat back in his seat.

"Oh. Well, thank you." Her cheeks flushed.

Was she feeling the same muddled mix of emotions as he was? Was her mind dancing around all the what-ifs? Had she missed him even a tenth as much as he'd missed her? "It's so weird being here together again."

She squeezed more ketchup from a plastic dispenser onto her plate and swirled a fry into the tangy sauce. "It is. This place, this food, even the updated jukebox, is so much like old times that for a second, it felt like we were still together."

"Maybe we should be." He shrugged, as if he wasn't asking her a question with that statement. "I remember a lot of wonderful times."

She picked up her pen and the notepad. "And I remember that your main goal is arresting my grandfather. So let's go back to discussing the one thing we do agree on—finding out what happened to Richard Harrington."

Chapter Five

Mia walked into Three Sisters Grindhouse and immediately felt like she'd come home. The scents of roasting coffee and freshly baked scones wafted up to greet her. Chloe and Julia were behind the counter, talking to each other, and even though she'd just seen her sisters last week, being in their presence again warmed her heart. And gave her something else to focus on other than the case and the confusing emotions going to lunch with Raylan had awakened.

"Mia!" Chloe came bustling around the counter and grabbed her sister in a tight hug. "What a surprise! I thought we weren't going to see you again until tomorrow night. How's Grandpa? Are you hungry? Do you want some coffee?"

Mia laughed. "Great, no and oh, please, yes."

Julia's hug was less enthusiastic, more guarded. Mia expected that. After all, Mia had been the one to leave them, to go off on her own instead of helping keep the coffee shop open after their grandmother died. Their relationship had been stiff and stilted ever since.

Mia had spent a lifetime trying to live up to the example set by her sisters. Julia, the oldest, had become a successful occupational therapist specializing in children who had gone through trauma. Chloe had taken over the family coffee shop and made it even more successful than it had been under their grandmother. Mia had been the one who'd barely graduated high school, avoided college and scraped by for several years in New York City while she figured out what she wanted to be when she grew up. Now she had a thriving business with her YouTube channel and a reputation in New York for being a dogged investigator. In Crooked Valley, though, she was still the Beaumont sister who had yet to make something of herself, especially to her sisters.

The day after she arrived in Crooked Valley, Mia had gone to Chloe's for dinner. Chloe had been overjoyed to see her middle sister and introduce Mia to eighteen-month-old William, who was a busy, walking, babbling bundle of joy. Julia and her new husband, Mike Byrne, were there as well with Mike's six-year-old daughter, Ginny, and their new baby, Emily. The dinner had been noisy and chaotic and absolutely wonderful, except for Julia's stubbornness in welcoming Mia back into the family fold. There'd been tension in the air, but the noise and happiness of the kids helped abate some of it.

Throughout it all, Mia had felt an odd sense of envy, as if this was the life she'd wanted all along. Once she got back to New York City, she was sure that feeling would evaporate.

"Glad you stopped by." Julia stepped back. Awkward silence filled the space.

For so long, Mia had felt like the one Beaumont girl who didn't fit. She didn't have Julia's drive or Chloe's warmth. She hadn't aced calculus or been elected homecoming queen. She'd ridden in the middle lane all through childhood and school, never standing out, never becoming the kid whose work was tacked on the fridge. Yes, her show was successful and made enough money to pay her bills and travel, but somehow, that didn't feel like enough.

"I know I haven't been back home much—"

"Two days at Christmas two years ago is less than much," Julia muttered, interrupting Mia.

"But I've missed you guys. I can hardly believe both of you got married and had kids. My sisters are *moms* now. It's so weird. But also kind of wonderful."

Julia arched a brow. "Says the sister who vowed she would never have children."

"I appreciate my nieces and nephews. I'm not running out to adopt one of my own." Mia laughed. The idea of her settling down like her sisters had and having kids seemed so foreign and yet that odd sense of jealousy had kept tingling in the back of her head ever since dinner at Chloe's. "Anyway, if you could pour me some coffee, I wanted to catch you up on Grandpa's case."

Talking about an investigation was where Mia felt confident and sure. It was like she was holding up a little sign for her sisters that said I Turned Out All Right. Please Be Proud of Me. She knew she shouldn't care what her family thought about her career, but she did. A lot.

"I saw something on the news about them finding a body on the property." Chloe poured Mia a cup of strong, rich coffee and added a splash of creamer. "Was it Richard?"

"It's complicated," Mia said. The three of them sat at the round table near the front door. Sun streamed through the plate-glass windows, casting a backward shadow of *Three Sisters Grindhouse* on the wood floor of the coffee shop. A mirror covered the wall behind the counter, with glass shelves full of bright white coffee cups, matching small plates, clear jars of loose teas and a few kitschy souvenirs with the store logo on them. The same wooden barstools lined the side of the counter, and the same plush mismatched love seats and low tables filled the rest of the shop. Three Sisters Grindhouse had been caught in a time warp since 1972, with only a touch-up of paint on the walls and a pair of shiny new espresso machines behind the counter. Once upon a time, Mia had thought that was boring and suffocating. Now she found the sameness comforting and…nice.

"Complicated how?" Julia took a sip of coffee.

"Raylan says the police think it's the body of Danielle, Richard and Grandpa's assistant. She was supposed to have moved away from Crooked Valley two weeks before Richard disappeared. But there's no evidence that she did or didn't move away. The cops barely followed up and never actually tracked her down."

Chloe sighed. "Finding another body doesn't exactly clear Grandpa as a suspect. Because the police will say he could have killed Danielle, too."

Mia nodded. "Even though we all know Grandpa would never kill anyone, the police are undoubtedly looking at him as a suspect again."

"Is there anything we can do to help? A witness we could find or anything?"

Wow. Julia asking to help? That was a nice surprise. Mia shook her head. "After thirty years, I'm not even sure *who* we should be looking for as witnesses. Besides, you two have busy lives with kids and husbands and this shop. Just keep an ear out for anything someone might say about the case." People who frequented little places like Three Sisters Grindhouse tended to chat, and maybe there'd be some gossip that could lead the case down a new path. "Either way, I think we should all spend extra time with Grandpa to keep his spirits up."

"Good idea. We'll see everyone tomorrow night and you can let me know what other nights work for you and Grandpa, Mia," Chloe said.

"I can invite everyone over on Sunday." Julia

smiled. "It's Mike's only full day off from his veterinary practice so I usually spoil him with a big dinner. He'd love to see the family again and talk about something other than cats and dogs, I'm sure."

"That all sounds great. And much better than me attempting to cook." Mia laughed. Grandpa Louis would undoubtedly be charmed by all the baby cuteness, and hopefully, it would take his mind off the case for a little while. Mia didn't like seeing him as worried as he had been this week. She'd done a few more interviews with him, but Grandpa Louis's excitement from the other day had disappeared. As time dragged on, he seemed to be almost waiting for the cops to show up on his doorstep with handcuffs.

"So...you mentioned Raylan Westfield." Chloe plopped her chin in her hands and raised a brow. "Anything we should know? Like, are you two getting back together?"

Julia rolled her eyes. "Chloe is still a hopeless romantic."

"Maybe so, but I was right about you and Mike Byrne, and now you two are happily married." Chloe grinned. "Who says Mia can't find her happily-ever-after with Raylan?"

Mia put her hands up. "Whoa. No one else in this family is getting married or falling in love or riding off into the sunset with their true love. I'm here to help Grandpa, and that's it. Raylan is just a means to an end, nothing more."

"Uh-huh." Chloe gathered the empty mugs and got

to her feet. "I don't believe that for a second. You've always had a thing for him."

"That was when I was eighteen. I'm older and wiser now. And not interested in falling in love with anyone." Except being with him at the diner had made her feel like a nervous teenager all over again. Ever since she arrived in Crooked Valley, she'd worried about whether Raylan thought she looked pretty, if he still found her interesting and whether he still cared about her. All senseless thoughts, since she was going back to New York after all this was over.

"Seems to me Julia said the same thing about not falling in love with anyone just before Christmas last year, and look at her now. Married, new baby, blissfully happy." Chloe shrugged. "Just saying."

"Chloe has a point about me saying I didn't want to fall in love. Then I did, and it has been...wonderful," Julia said.

"And if you fell in love with Raylan again, then you could stay in Crooked Valley," Chloe added with a grin.

This was why Mia avoided coming home—to escape these kinds of conversations. Mia threw on her coat and crossed to the door. "Sorry, girls, but I have to get back to work on the case. I'll bring Grandpa over tomorrow night."

"Bring Raylan, too," Chloe said as Mia pushed on the handle to open the door. "I bet that man would love a home-cooked meal."

Mia ignored Chloe's clear attempt at matchmaking, said goodbye to her sisters and headed out into the Crooked Valley sunshine. Before she had a moment to enjoy the warmth, her phone buzzed with a text from Raylan: We need to talk. Now.

Raylan had debated giving Mia a heads-up before they pulled Louis in for questioning. If it had been anyone else, he wouldn't have made the call. Did that mean he was showing favoritism toward the Beaumonts? Or just feeling some sympathy for someone else whose family name had been damaged by Harrington's disappearance?

He'd texted Mia to ask her to meet him at the property so he could show her why the suspicion was now leaning in her grandfather's direction. Hugh had made it clear that he thought Louis Beaumont had something to do with Harrington's disappearance and that it was high time the police took another crack at him.

Mia was not going to be happy to hear that, not one bit. Raylan knew that with Mia, the only way to make her understand was with concrete proof, and in this case, they had a lot of that. The techs had pulled down the crime-scene tape this afternoon, except for one long strand attached to the front porch that whipped around from time to time in the breeze. The CVPD's second search had been extensive and thorough, running long into the night and starting again early this morning. They'd covered the same ground as they had thirty years ago, combing through every nook and cranny of Harrington's property.

But this time, they also brought cadaver dogs.

Mia's car pulled into the driveway and parked behind his car. As she walked toward him, Raylan steeled himself for the conversation they were about to have and wrestled with whether any of this was a good idea because he was far from an impartial party.

Today she had her hair pulled back in a ponytail and was wearing an oversized pale pink sweatshirt under her coat, a casual pairing with her faded jeans. It reminded him of when they'd fallen in love in high school and his every thought revolved around her. Yet again, another reason why he should pull himself out of this equation. Hugh could oversee it just as easily.

Except Hugh didn't know Mia. Even though Raylan could see the evidence stacking up against her grandfather, there was some reason deep inside him that kept him from walking away, both from the mystery and from her.

"What happened?" She locked her car and pocketed the keys. "Did they find something?"

"Yes, but it's more than that. I want to show you something." He motioned for her to follow him. They crossed the property, passing the carriage house and stopping in front of the well.

Mia scowled at the footprints in the mud around the stone. "I was going to search this well on the first day, and now it seems the cops already have."

"If you had, you would have found Danielle's husband." He was glad it had been the dogs that had alerted the cops to this well, instead of Mia finding another skeleton. No matter how often a person saw a dead body, it never got easier, and he was grateful he could save her that trauma.

Mia put a hand to her mouth. "Oh, no. He was killed, too?"

Raylan nodded. "Bullet wound to the temple, same as Danielle, and a second one to his chest. Because the body is skeletal, the coroner can't rule out suicide, but he thinks it's very unlikely that her husband shot himself twice and then fell to the bottom of a well. There was no gun found with the body, either, and nothing found in the ground around the well. It's pretty impossible for someone to kill themselves and then toss away the gun. It could have been found by kids or something over the years, but the police department thinks that's unlikely. Which means this was a murder, too." He watched Mia's face as he talked, searching for any telltale signs that she knew something. If she and her grandfather were working together to solve this case, it was possible Louis knew who murdered Danielle and Paul.

Mia, however, looked as surprised as anyone about the news, so it was possible she didn't know anything. The more time Raylan spent with her, the more he prayed her grandfather wasn't the murderer. Which was reason number 722 why Raylan shouldn't be working on this case with Mia.

"And no trace of Harrington?" Mia's gaze swept

the property, as if the financier's body would magically appear.

"No." Raylan shook his head. "The—"

A sharp boom erupted, followed by something whizzing past Raylan's ear. Both of them froze for a split second, stunned, puzzling it out—the sound made no sense in the serene woods. But then, the gears clicked in Raylan's mind, and he grabbed Mia's arm just before a second boom came. "Run!"

They dashed toward her car, Mia fumbling with the keys as she ran and pressing the unlock button over and over again. Two more bullets whizzed by them in quick succession, coming close enough to graze Raylan's wool sleeve and tear a hole in the hood of Mia's coat. Whoever was shooting was clearly aiming for both of them. In an unspoken agreement, Raylan headed for the driver's side and Mia dove into the passenger side. Why? And who?

They could find those answers later. After he got Mia someplace safe.

"Get down, Mia!" Raylan pressed the button to start the car, slammed it into Reverse as soon as the engine caught and zipped down the driveway, just as a bullet hit the driver's rear window. "Call 911!"

Mia's hands were shaking so much it took her two tries to get the numbers punched into her phone. "We're at the Harrington estate and River Rock Road," she told the operator. "Someone is inside the house shooting at me and the assistant district attorney. No, we're not hurt. But they're still shooting."

The next shot pinged off the wheel well, and another kicked up the dirt alongside the passenger side.

Raylan kept his foot on the pedal until they reached the end of the long, long driveway. It was nearly a mile, far enough that he doubted the shooter would follow. He could hear the sirens already and see the faint sparkle of blue-and-red lights in the distance.

Raylan backed the car into the woods along the side of the road, hiding it at the same time he aimed the nose toward the driveway so they could see if anyone was coming behind them. He kept the car running, just in case, but doubted anyone would be foolish to come any closer when the police were thirty seconds away.

Raylan opened the driver's-side door. "Stay inside and stay low," he told Mia, who was still crammed into the space beneath the dash. "I'm going to see if I see anything."

He took a cautious step out of the car and ducked down beside the front quarter panel. He scanned the road, the driveway, the woods, but didn't see or hear anything except the sound of sirens getting closer and closer. The CVPD arrived moments later. Mia got out of the car, and the two of them gave what little they knew to the police officers.

"Stay here," one of the deputies said. "We'll search the property." He motioned to another officer to remain with them.

Raylan gathered Mia in a hug. "Are you sure you're okay?" He pulled back, and his gaze swept over her, looking for blood, a scratch, anything. If Mia had been hurt—

"I'm fine." Her eyes were wide, but her features were full of strength and determination. "What about you?"

"I'm okay, too. All I have is a hole in my favorite coat." Raylan held out the sleeve of the thick wool overcoat and then reached for Mia's hood. "And there's a hole in yours."

She peered over her shoulder at the tear, and he saw her shiver. "He came very close to hitting us."

"Maybe on purpose." The shooter had missed them by mere inches. Was that by accident or by design? It seemed that he'd had the advantage and could have easily killed them and yet…here they were, alive and well.

"Who was that out there?" Mia whispered.

"I wish I knew." Raylan stayed close to her, resisting the urge to tell Mia to go home, lock the door and stay far, far away from this place. They paced while they waited what seemed like hours before the other officers returned.

"There's no sign of anyone on the property," a younger officer named Brooks said. "But there is evidence that someone has been inside the house, maybe for hours. We found some empty food wrappers and a blanket. Neither of those things were there when we concluded our search."

That information sent a shiver up Raylan's spine.

"That means someone broke into the empty mansion after you were done searching it again," Mia said. "Why?"

In thirty years, no one had visited this property except for the police. And now, the day Raylan and Mia came back, there was a shooter inside? That was too much of a coincidence. "I think it's worse than that. I think someone knew we were coming and was waiting for a chance to shoot us." Worry tightened in Raylan's chest. Who had known he was meeting Mia here? The only person he'd told was Susan, and she was the most trustworthy person he knew. How did the information get out?

"Or maybe someone has been watching us all along." Mia pointed at the thick woods that ringed Harrington's mansion, and Raylan got the strangest sense she was holding something back. "Anyone could hide in there for days and not be noticed."

Raylan turned back to the young deputy, who had been part of the bigger search last night and this morning. If anyone knew details about what they found, it would be this guy. "Brooks, did the officers search the woods around the property when they were here yesterday?"

"No, sir. They aren't part of the estate, and our orders were to search this property only."

That was part of what Raylan loved and hated about the law—the preciseness of it. They had stuck to the acreage previously owned by Harrington and ignored everything else, on orders. "Well, I think we need to search them now."

"Already on it, sir. The chief is assembling teams as we speak." Brooks nodded at Mia's car. "If you want, sir, I can have your vehicle brought up so you and Miss Beaumont can leave. Just know that we might call you two in for questioning later."

"Sounds good. I appreciate that." Raylan could have gotten the car himself but couldn't bear the thought of leaving Mia unguarded for even a second. As soon as she went home, he knew he would worry. If the shooter had been lying in wait for them, there was no telling how desperate he would get or whether he would show up at their houses.

All that led to one question: Why was the case of a man who had disappeared three decades ago suddenly becoming so dangerous? Was it possible that Harrington was alive, as Louis had been saying for years, and had shot at them to cover his tracks?

Beside him, Mia started shivering and wrapped her arms tightly around herself, despite her thick winter coat. The temperature had dropped, but Raylan suspected the chill she was feeling was from fear. She watched the woods as if she expected the shooter to come charging out at any moment. "To think that we were being watched…"

"Or tracked." Raylan took off his jacket and draped it over Mia's shoulders, an extra layer and a way to tell her it would be okay, although what he really wanted to do was hold her tight to his chest and never let her go. The jacket would have to suffice for the comfort he wanted to give. She snuggled into the thick fabric and thanked him. "Who knew you were coming here?"

"Only my grandfather. I called him to tell him I'd be late getting to his house because I was meeting you first."

"Your grandfather knew you were meeting me?" Yet another piece of the puzzle that tied in Louis Beaumont with the Harrington disappearance. But Louis was in his late seventies. There was no way he had shot at them. Was there?

Mia cocked her head, as if she was reading his mind. "Come on, Raylan. You don't seriously think my grandfather was hiding up in that house shooting at us, do you?"

"I don't know. Anything's possible."

"Well, that is definitely not possible. He wouldn't do that. He couldn't do that."

In the years he'd been with the district attorney's office, Raylan had seen a lot of things that didn't seem possible. The people you least suspected sometimes turned out to be the most vicious criminals. "Does your grandfather own a rifle?"

"Are you questioning me?" Her gaze narrowed. "Wait. You didn't just ask me to meet you here to see the well. You wanted to *interrogate* me."

Everything had suddenly gone sideways. The warm conversations between them had chilled like the air, and everything in her body language was defensive, angry. "It's not like that, Mia. I wanted to show you the well, yes, but I wanted to tell you—"

"Tell me what, Raylan? That this was all a way for you to get more information? For you to disrupt my investigation? For you to—"

"To tell you that Detective Morales has brought your grandfather in for questioning." There. The truth was out, and there was no way he could bring it back. "But it does mean there's no way he could be the shooter."

"Of course he's not the shooter. Because my grandfather is *not a murderer.*" Anger ignited in her features. She shrugged out of his jacket and shoved it into his hands. "Were you trying to get me out of the way so you could have my grandfather arrested? This whole thing was a way to make sure I didn't get in the way."

Even he could see how the timing seemed intentional. All Raylan had wanted was the opportunity to explain what was happening in person so that Mia wouldn't worry about her grandfather. "Questioning witnesses is a normal part of the process, Mia. I—"

"I don't want to hear it. Anything else you have to say to me, Raylan, should probably be said through a lawyer." She got in her car, put it in gear and took off, leaving a trail of dirt and dust in her wake.

Chapter Six

Mia paced the lobby of the Crooked Valley Police Department, walking the perimeter of the small space so many times that she was surprised she didn't wear the finish off the tiles. It seemed like her grandfather had been in the interrogation room for hours and hours. She'd asked the desk sergeant a hundred times if she could go back there and be there with her grandfather, but he refused to allow her any farther into the building.

The police are questioning Grandpa right now, Mia texted her sisters.

There was a flurry of texts exchanged between the three girls, with Chloe sounding worried and Julia asking Mia what she had done to get their grandfather arrested. Typical. Chloe, the youngest, was concerned about Mia's and Grandpa's welfare, while Julia was blaming her middle sister for what happened.

Finally, a little after six, she heard a door open and saw Grandpa coming down the hall. As soon as he came through the lobby door, she grabbed him in a tight hug. "I'm so sorry."

He patted her back. "It's okay. I'm fine. Just talked out."

"Let's get you home then." She crooked her grandfather's arm into hers and helped him out of the station, down the granite steps and over to the parking lot. He seemed exhausted but only mildly irritated by the interruption to his day. Once he was settled in the passenger seat, Mia whispered a thank-you to God for her grandfather's good spirits. Maybe the questioning hadn't been as brutal as she'd imagined.

Mia picked up takeout on the way to her grandfather's house, then got him settled in his favorite chair while she dished them up some Chinese food. She opted for the chicken stir-fry while Grandpa got his favorite sweet-and-sour chicken. She curled up on the couch, only a few feet away from him, casting glances at him from time to time as they ate and *Jeopardy!* played in the background. She didn't dare broach the subject of the questioning in case it upset her elderly grandfather.

"I see you staring at me. I'm fine. It was just a few questions."

More than a few, given how many hours he'd been back there. "I think it was wrong of them to drag you down to the station, Grandpa. You should have at least called a lawyer."

"Why? I have nothing to hide. I want this solved as much as the police do."

She'd seen way too many cases where people hadn't opted to call a lawyer and had ended up in jail. Not that she was disparaging the Crooked Valley Police Department, but if her grandfather was already on their suspect list, anything he said could be interpreted as something that could be used against him. Grandpa Louis put far too much trust into other people. "I know. But I think the police want different answers than you do."

"I know that." Her grandfather sighed and set his half-eaten bowl on the end table. "I was sorry to hear about Danielle and Paul. All these years, I thought they were living a new life in Grand Rapids. I can't believe they never made it there."

"You never reached out?"

Her grandfather shook his head. "I was busy, running the business and then trying to recover after it all came crashing down. I should have, but I didn't. I just assumed…"

"Yeah." She could hear the regret in his voice and see the sadness in the slump of his shoulders. The entire case was getting stranger by the minute, with surprises she hadn't seen coming. The discovery of the bodies. The shooter inside the house who had nearly hit Raylan and Mia. The stranger watching her when she left the Harrington estate the other day. A stranger who could also be trying to kill her and Raylan?

Someone didn't want Mia getting close to the truth, but who that someone was, Mia had no idea. She debated telling her grandfather about the shooter but decided he'd had more than enough stress for one day. She didn't want him worrying about her, and especially not as much as she was worrying about herself and Raylan.

Even though the police thought her grandfather was a suspect, Mia had another person in mind for this increasingly confusing mystery. But that someone had been gone for decades and wasn't the man she'd seen in the driveway. Still, she asked the question. "Grandpa, do you think Richard had anything to do with the deaths of Danielle and Paul?"

"I don't know, Mia." Her grandfather let out a long, heavy sigh. "I just don't know."

The next day, Raylan and his boss, Hugh Levine, had watched most of the video of the interrogation of Louis Beaumont, hoping to catch some kind of clue or direction for the case. While Louis had answered every single question, he hadn't revealed anything that law enforcement didn't already know about the Harrington case. "Either Beaumont is very good at lying or he truly doesn't know anything," Hugh said.

"He did seem surprised to find out that Danielle and Paul had been murdered," Raylan replied.

"Maybe. A lot of people suddenly become very good actors when their neck is on the line." Hugh got to his feet. The DA was a tall man with a wiry build who kept himself trim with daily runs. "I think we need to stir the pot a little more."

Raylan leaned back in the creaky office chair in the conference room. "Stir the pot? What do you mean by that?"

"I think your father was right. I think Beaumont is good for this disappearance, maybe even murder. And I think we should make our position very, very clear to him."

A chill ran through Raylan. "You're talking about having a press conference."

Hugh slipped on his overcoat. They'd spent the latter half of the day going through the tape and talking about the case. Hugh had the experience that Raylan lacked, and Raylan had hoped Hugh would provide some guidance and direction, but this wasn't the direction he'd expected.

"I think it's time we let Beaumont know we're onto him. That we never, in fact, thought he was innocent. The man's in poor health. It's possible he'll confess just to get it off his chest."

"But what about the shooting? Louis was at the police station when that happened. There's no way he was a part of that."

Hugh shrugged. "Doesn't matter. Beaumont had something to do with Harrington's disappearance. I'm convinced of that, especially after seeing his interview. Let's make him sweat and maybe he'll break."

Raylan nodded as Hugh left, but didn't feel the

agreement in his soul. Yes, it was entirely possible for Louis Beaumont to have killed Harrington to get the money—he definitely had a motive. But to be involved with the shooting of his own granddaughter? That stretched credulity.

Raylan had little doubt that someone out there didn't want the ADA or a YouTube investigator to get close to the truth. Every crime had multiple layers to it, and with this much money, there could be someone else involved who had stayed under the radar of law enforcement. Could Louis have an accomplice? Someone younger who could run from the police and disappear into the woods? Someone with good enough aim to barely miss shooting Mia?

If so, what on earth could that accomplice be trying to keep them from discovering? There'd been several thorough searches of the Harrington property, including the woods near the mansion, and the searches hadn't found any other trace of the shooter, the money or clues to Harrington's whereabouts. It was unlikely that the CVPD had left any stones unturned. Yet, there was still one body missing.

Richard's.

Whoever was involved with the disappearance of the millionaire investor would want to cover his or her tracks. Was that what the shooter was trying to do?

As Raylan had reminded the DA, Louis had a rock-solid alibi for the shooting, which meant he could be ruled out as the one pulling the trigger. But his alibi for the day Harrington disappeared wasn't so solid and didn't clear him as a suspect. It was entirely possible that Louis had snuck out and committed the crime while his wife thought he was home sick, or that his wife would lie to protect her husband and cover for his misdeeds. Either way, Hugh clearly had seen guilt in that interview.

Raylan rewound the tape until he got to the section that had left him with some nagging doubts. "Mr. Beaumont," Morales said to the elderly Louis in the video, "was it true that Richard Harrington disappeared with more than three million dollars in cash?"

Louis Beaumont looked composed and calm, his demeanor seeming cooperative and patient with the endless questioning. Morales had taken a more combative stance, but the other man seemed unfazed and nodded before he replied. "Richard took all of the money the company had invested for our clients. Every last dime. So many people were completely wiped out."

"And so were you. When he emptied that bank account, it was your money as well."

"It was *all* of my money." Louis leaned forward, and for the first time, Raylan saw the older man show tension in his face, maybe even anger. Could he be hiding a deeper rage about what Richard Harrington had done? "For months, we had been earning excellent returns on our investments, and I thought it would be a good idea to invest more in our company, so I poured all of my savings into the firm and gave

Richard the reins because he seemed so much better at investing than I was. The stocks I chose earned maybe eight percent a year. Richard's returns were closer to fifteen, twenty percent. I saw the clients getting richer, and frankly, I wanted some of that wealth in my own pocket, too." Louis sighed. "I was greedy, and because of that greed, I ended up penniless."

"Greedy, huh?" Morales leaned over the table. "So greedy that you'd kill your assistant, her husband and your business partner so you could steal the money back from Harrington?"

Louis tensed. He might not have even been aware of the way his spine straightened and his shoulders rose, but the camera saw everything, and Raylan could see the question had upset the older man. "I spent three years trying to recoup what I lost financially. My family struggled for a long time. Do you really think that would have happened if I'd had the money Richard stole?"

Morales leaned back in his chair and shrugged. "Maybe Harrington wouldn't tell you where it was and you killed him out of frustration."

"I've never killed anyone," Louis said. "I suffered just as much as our clients did after Richard disappeared. I had nothing to do with whatever happened to him."

Raylan clicked off the tape. Louis seemed earnest and honest enough in his answers, but there was one word Raylan kept circling back to: *greedy.* "I was greedy," Louis had said. Greedy enough to kill?

Today, the elderly man looked too frail to be a killer, but thirty years ago, he would have been younger, faster, stronger and maybe more willing to take a risk if it meant securing his family's future. Raylan had learned long ago that some of the most innocent-looking people committed some of the most heinous crimes. What he needed now was more evidence.

Mia wanted to clear her grandfather, and Hugh clearly wanted to put him in jail. Raylan needed to find the missing pieces that could finally put this mystery to rest. And Raylan would have solved the one crime that had haunted his father long after he left office.

Bringing closure to the Harrington case could very well come at the cost of breaking Mia's heart. Could Raylan live with that?

He shelved those thoughts. There was maybe two hours of daylight left today. Even though it was foolish, and Raylan was sure the chief would kill him for doing this, Raylan headed back over to the Harrington property. Maybe there was something that the officers missed, some clue they'd overlooked. The multiple searches conducted by the CVPD made that unlikely, but Raylan needed to be active, and see that forward progress was being made on this case. It was the only way any of them, Mia included, could sleep at night.

There was also a part of him that wanted to find the shooter who had threatened Mia's life. There was only one way to ensure that he would never see that look of fear on her face again. Arrest the person responsible and put them in prison for a very, very long time.

As he drove, he flipped on the radio, tuning it to a local Crooked Valley radio station. As he did, he heard Hugh's voice, loud and clear, in an interview he must have just given outside the office. "We are reopening the investigation of the disappearance of Richard Harrington. And as part of that reopening, we are looking at any suspects we might have had thirty years ago."

A female reporter piped up first. "Does that list include Louis Beaumont?"

Raylan held his breath in the pause before Hugh answered. He prayed Hugh would keep everything confidential, that he would give the CVPD time to investigate before pointing the finger. "It's a very short list," Hugh said. "And, yes, Beaumont is on it."

Raylan flipped off the radio and shook his head. What was it about this case that had made his father—and now Hugh—rush to judgment? Was it the high stakes with all the missing money? Was it fame?

Or was Raylan just too close to the prime suspect's granddaughter to see the truth?

He parked in the Harrington driveway and took a moment to survey the grounds before stepping out of his car. The property was quiet, barely a bird or a squirrel making noise. The silence was eerie, and

Raylan half expected to hear the report of a rifle. But there was nothing.

Yes, there was a slim chance that whoever had shot at them was back here again. The shooter would have to be an idiot to come back to a place the police had searched, which was why Raylan figured this was the best time to satisfy his own curiosity. Plus, no one knew Raylan was coming here. In an abundance of caution, he hadn't even mentioned it to Susan. Raylan was hoping that the perpetrator had been reckless enough to leave behind something that would identify him, something investigators overlooked.

The front door of the house was open, and a scattering of leaves covered the long hallway. The fancy artwork and fine furniture that had once gleamed in these rooms was coated with dust, most of it undisturbed by vandals or animals, and the home had a haunted, empty feeling that seemed so tragic and sad. It was as if the entire house was caught in a time warp—a preserved photograph of the moment Richard Harrington disappeared.

If only the dust and leaves could paint a picture of what happened, but the property had been too disrupted by the searches to leave any clues behind. Enough officers had been through the house to confuse any footprints that might have been there. The wind had done the rest.

Raylan clicked on the light for his phone. He'd forgotten to bring a flashlight—Mia would have remembered because Mia was that kind of woman who always remembered the details—and the daylight streaming through the two front windows didn't reach into the farthest corners. The plywood covering them the last time Raylan was here had been removed by the search team and stacked neatly against the wall. A faint gray powder covered both window frames, but no fingerprints had been found, as Morales had told Raylan. The shooter had been smart enough to wear gloves. Raylan ducked down, shining the light into the corners, hoping against hope that he'd find an overlooked clue.

"What are you doing here?"

He jumped, then turned at the sound of Mia's voice. "You startled me."

"Sorry." She stepped inside, took off her hat and stuffed it into her coat pocket. The sun illuminated her from behind, dancing off the golden highlights in her hair. "I didn't know you'd be at the house today."

That meant she'd intended to come here alone, even after all that had happened with the shooter. "You were going to search this place alone? Mia, that's too risky."

She arched a brow. "Pretty sure that's what you're doing, am I right?"

"Touché." Just because he was a man didn't make him any less vulnerable to a bullet. He was, admittedly, a little relieved that he'd been here when she arrived because then she wouldn't be alone on these expansive grounds. At least he'd be here to protect her if anything happened, or hopefully do a better job of keeping her out of harm's way than he had yesterday. He motioned toward the room. "Maybe we should work together? Get it done in half the time?"

"Absolutely not." Her features hardened, and she shook her head. "After you had the cops interrogate my grandfather? And then the DA gave a *press conference* naming my grandfather as a suspect? What are you two trying to do? Destroy what family I have left?"

"No, of course not." The heartbreak and betrayal in her face made him wonder if Hugh was rushing to close a case. No. Raylan had seen the tape himself. Louis had said he was greedy. The DA had to go down every possible path, and right now, that path led to Louis. Still, Raylan hated to see her hurt.

"I don't want to work with you because I know if we find any evidence, you'll use it to pin the whole thing on my grandpa." Her eyes filled with tears, but her resolve kept them from falling. "I thought I knew you, Raylan. Thought I could trust you."

"Mia—"

She threw up her hands and the moment of emotion disappeared. "I can't have this conversation. In fact, I can't have *any* conversations with you because as the old Miranda rights say, you can and will use it against me, or worse, against my elderly grandfather, who has lung cancer." She spun away and headed outside.

He knew he should let her go. She had, after all,

many good reasons to be upset with him. If the roles had been reversed, he wouldn't have spoken to her at all, he was sure. Not that he could blame her, because both of them were here for similar reasons: to protect their families and help them find the answers they needed. How could he possibly be upset that she felt betrayed?

Raylan had seen the pain in her face, the worry in the slump of her shoulders, and that had him following her outside. It didn't matter if she rebuffed him or screamed at him. He hadn't called the press conference, and he hadn't made the police department's suspicions public knowledge, but that didn't matter to Mia. She was suffering. Raylan had never been able to stand seeing Mia upset and, worse, being part of the reason for her misery. Even more so now that they were both adults who had weathered painful storms. There was a part of him that had never really stopped loving her, and that was the part that wanted to offer some kind of comfort.

She was walking fast, crossing the thick, grassy yard at a quick pace, and he had to hustle to close the gap. "Mia, wait!"

Either she didn't hear him or didn't want to wait for him, because she kept going. Raylan broke into a light jog and caught up with her. "I'm sorry."

She stopped short and spun toward him. "For what? For having my grandfather arrested? For putting an elderly man through an interrogation? For calling a senior citizen a suspect in a crime he had nothing to do with? A senior citizen who is very ill, might I remind you?"

Guilt washed over Raylan. He'd been doing his job, following his boss's orders, when he'd had Louis questioned, but to hear it put in those terms made him seem like some unfeeling monster. "I don't want to add any more stress to your grandfather's life than he already has. But I can't ignore the evidence or skip asking the questions that will bring the truth into the light."

"Is it the truth, though? Or is it what you and the DA want the truth to be?" She raised a hand to stop him from speaking again. He could see the frustration written all over her, mingled with hurt and betrayal. "It doesn't matter. I don't have time for this or you. I need to prove my grandfather's innocence before you throw him into jail."

She started walking again. Raylan debated going back to his search of the house and avoiding the tension between them. That would be the coward's way out, the way a younger, more immature Raylan would have handled things. He'd let Mia get away when they were younger, instead of telling her how much losing her would break his heart. He'd spent the past twelve years wondering about her, missing her, and as much as he would love a second chance, he knew the investigative mountain between them was insurmountable.

But he could protect her and support her and help

her. He tagged along behind her, ignoring the glares she shot over her shoulder.

"I don't need your help, Raylan."

"Yes, you do, Mia." He didn't want to tell her he was worried about her being alone on the property after what had happened yesterday, because she would undoubtedly reassure him that twelve years living in New York City had made her pretty impervious to fear. And he also didn't want to tell her that he was here because he cared deeply about her and knew it would be foolish to tell her how he felt. Instead, he scrambled for a reason that seemed at least somewhat plausible. "Because I know something about these woods that you don't."

She kept walking but her pace slowed. "What are you talking about?"

"You brought me in because I know the history of this town. And that historical background means I might know a place where there might be a building that a shooter can hide out in."

Her steps faltered, and she shot Raylan a quick, concerned glance. "I thought he was hiding in the house."

"I think he wanted us to believe that. I got into the house and started thinking about how neatly arranged the evidence was. I think the shooter was hiding somewhere else so he could watch people come and go. When he saw us there, he snuck up to the house to take a shot."

She gestured at the expanse of woods, which were thinning by the day as fall moved toward winter and the trees shed their leaves. "Where would he hide? There's a landscaper's shed on the property, right? In there?"

"That caved in years ago, so it wouldn't make for a very warm vantage point in this weather. I think he's somewhere we wouldn't think to look. Somewhere a little deeper into the woods than the police probably went."

"Where?" Mia scanned the thick woods, so quiet and eerie on this cold day. They'd had a warmish day yesterday, which had erased the light dusting of snow that had been on the ground. Any footprints there might have been were erased, but Raylan knew the path.

"Follow me." Raylan started into the forest. Mia hesitated, then fell into step behind him. Every few seconds, Raylan paused to make sure he was going the right way. The clues were there, but they had faded over the last century. A broken stump here, a mark on a tree there. Then, finally, a pile of rocks sitting beside a rotted fallen tree, looking like a kid had dumped their findings in one place, but Raylan knew it was more. He skirted the tree, stepping carefully.

"What are you looking for?"

"In 1917, pretty much every town and city in Colorado got on the Prohibition bandwagon…except for Denver. The city resisted instituting a liquor ban until the end of 1918, when the supporters of Prohibition argued that the grain crops were better used to feed the country than to intoxicate the country.

Things around here were already lean because of the war, and that just sealed the vote for the supporters."

"What does any of that have to do with Richard Harrington and my grandfather?"

Raylan brushed at some leaves. Pushed a fallen branch out of the way. He moved slowly and carefully, in a gradually widening circle around the pile of rocks. "Moonshiners were active in these woods and had a number of little cabins they built to stay at while they ran the still. One of those cabins still exists, and it's close enough to the Harrington property to be a good hiding place." Raylan bent down, swept aside some dirt and revealed a shiny, white quartz rock deep in the earth. "There it is."

"What?"

"The trail that leads to the cabin." He started walking through the woods, in the direction the tip of the rock had been pointed—it was a subtle clue that few people would recognize. The brush along the path was broken in many places, indicating that either a person or a large animal had been through here recently. Raylan kept his eyes on the ground, looking for the next quartz rock—which would give them their next turn. "The moonshiners used rocks, specifically white quartz, to mark the path."

"Because white rocks reflect any light that's shone on them."

"Exactly." He saw the next rock and took a right, and once again encountered a trail that had been used recently, given that the tall grass was flattened and the branches pushed out of the way. The markings were as clear as footprints. Raylan's heart rate accelerated, and his gaze swept the woods, looking for any sign of another person. "Eventually the cops figured out their system, and the stills were shut down, but it was a moot point because Prohibition was repealed a couple years later, in 1933. The cabins, however—" he pushed aside a thick pile of brush "—still exist."

And there it was, a tiny six-by-eight log cabin, covered in moss and leaves. The forest had nearly swallowed the entire building in its long arms of limbs and cloak of leaves. The trees formed a natural camouflage for the rustic, weather-beaten cabin. If they hadn't known it was there, it would have been easy for Raylan and Mia to walk right past it.

Mia started to move past him, and Raylan put out a hand to stop her. "We're not the only ones who know about this place," he whispered. He pointed at the cold remains of a fire in the makeshift firepit outside the cabin. "He may be in there right now. Let me check it out first."

"You don't have to be the big man taking care of me. I can take care of myself."

"I have no doubt of that, Mia. But that doesn't mean I'm going to let you walk in front of a rifle again. So, please, wait here for a second."

She rolled her eyes but did as he asked and stepped behind a large oak tree. Raylan moved forward, slowly, watching the cabin and the surrounding woods for any sense of movement. At the entrance he clicked on his phone's light again, bent down and peered around the open door, then swung the light across the interior. Nothing. There was no one inside, but Raylan had no doubt someone had been here very recently, based on the empty cans that littered the floor and the cast-iron pot with a few dried-out beans stubbornly clinging to the lip. He took one last long look at the woods and then gestured to Mia. "I think it's safe."

For now, he wanted to add but didn't. The cabin was small enough that any searching would only take a minute at most. Raylan didn't see much in the way of belongings—a black sweatshirt, a pair of gloves and an unopened box of rifle shells. He raised his phone to call the police, but this far into the woods and away from town, he saw no bars on the screen. They were cut off from safety and that thought caused a chill to run through him.

Whoever had been here surely wouldn't be back before they finished. Would they?

"We have to be quick in case someone comes back," Mia said, as if she'd read his mind.

"Don't touch anything. I can't get a signal to call the forensics team, but I'll try texting Morales. Hopefully that will get through." He dropped a pin and sent a photo to the detective. A second later, the screen said the text was undeliverable. "I think we should head back and then call. I don't want to be here any longer than necessary."

Mia picked up a stick and used it to push the sweatshirt around, revealing a thick black hood and white strings to tighten the neckline. "I feel like I've seen this sweatshirt before somewhere. I think—"

A twig snapped. Mia jerked up her head. Raylan spun toward the open door, just as he saw a figure dressed in black moving into the cover of the deep forest. "Get down!"

In some kind of nightmare on repeat, Raylan heard the report of a rifle at the same time a bullet whizzed past them and slammed into the wall. Another one, right after the first, but lower this time. Raylan put one arm around Mia and knocked the small table to the floor, tipping the top toward the door. The wooden square was no real protection, but it would have to do because the only way out of the window-less building was through the front door—the same direction the bullets were coming from.

Raylan glanced around the room, looking for a weapon, any kind of weapon. Empty soup cans. A heavy pot. Clothing. "The police are on their way!" he called out, a lie that he hoped would make the shooter run in the opposite direction.

The shooter's answer came in the form of a third bullet that skipped over the top of the table, sending a chunk of wood flying into Raylan's chest. He scrambled backward with Mia and the table, toward the corner that was beside the front door, out of sight, he prayed, of the shooter, but with enough of a vantage point to see him if he emerged from the woods. Raylan handed Mia his phone. "Do you remember how we got here?"

She nodded.

"I'm going to distract him, and when I do, I want you to run as far and as fast as you can. As soon as you get a signal, call Morales and tell him to hurry."

"What are you going to do?" Mia's eyes were wide.

Raylan twisted at the table leg, unscrewing the long, thin piece of wood from the top. He handed it to her and then picked up the cast-iron pan. "Stop whoever is shooting at us."

Chapter Seven

Mia tried to stop Raylan, but he escaped her grasp
before she could pull him back into the relative safety
of their little corner. Relative, because truly, they
weren't safe anywhere in this tiny space with only
one exit. She watched Raylan duck outside and prayed
harder than she'd ever prayed for anything in her life.
Please don't let him get hurt. Please protect him.

For the longest time she heard…nothing. No shots,
no voices. The lone sound of a bird tweeting from
somewhere just outside the cabin broke the silence
but then the forest quieted again. In those long moments while she waited, expecting to hear the boom
of a rifle at any second, a thousand emotions ran
through Mia. Fear, worry, anxiety.

And most of all, something that made Mia wonder
if her heart was completely closed to Raylan Westfield after all, because whatever was going through
her heart while she waited for him to—*please, God*—

come back safely from the woods wasn't friendship, but it wasn't quite love, either. It was something in between that she didn't have the time or emotional space to deal with.

When another couple of minutes went by without a sound, Mia climbed out from behind the table and peeked her head around the doorjamb, the table leg in her hands—it was a weapon she prayed she didn't have to get close enough to use. There was a crashing sound, breaking branches, leaves crunching, and Mia raised the table leg over her head, stepped forward and—

Raylan emerged from the woods, frustration written all over his face. "I think he's gone. I saw him take off into the trees when I came out. I tried to follow, but he had a good lead on me."

Thank God. She was so relieved to see him alive and well that she almost broke into tears. Raylan was safe, but they were no closer to answers about who was shooting at them than they had been yesterday.

"Do you think he meant to kill us?" Mia set the table leg on the floor of the cabin. Releasing the weight of it was like releasing the weight of her worry while Raylan was gone. Thank goodness, he was safe.

But who on earth would want to kill either of them? She was sure Raylan had made some enemies during his years in the prosecutor's office, but certainly not any that would want to murder him?

"No, I don't think so." Raylan closed the distance between them, tossing the cast-iron pan down. It landed with a heavy thud on the wooden floor. "Just like the first time, if he wanted to kill us, he could have. He had a perfect opportunity to shoot me when I went outside, but instead he retreated into the woods. I think he's trying to scare us off. Maybe distract us from the case."

She glanced up at Raylan's handsome face. He stood there, so tall and strong and brave for charging out there to protect them. His gaze stayed just above hers, locked on the woods, his stance at the ready to protect her, and something softened inside her. "I'm really glad you're safe, Raylan."

"I'm glad you're okay, too, Mia. But there's still someone out there shooting at us, and we have to find out who it is before he or she hurts someone."

For a moment, Mia didn't give a hoot about the case, the shooter or anything in the past. She moved closer to the man she used to love, waiting until his dark blue gaze dropped down to meet her own. She took his hands in hers and thought how right, how perfect, that felt. "I never stopped caring about you, you know." The admission slipped from her in one soft whisper.

There was a beat between them, a moment where whatever either of them said could open a door they had shut years ago, or close it even more firmly. Raylan's gaze softened and a slow smile spread across his face. "I never stopped caring about you, either, Mia. I was young and foolish back then, and if I could do it all over again…"

"What would you do?" she persisted when he didn't finish. She knew it would be foolish to get involved with him again, especially now, with her grandfather's future at stake and her eventual return to the city. Yet here in the woods, with no one else around them, and caught in the charged air of the danger they had escaped, she couldn't quite seem to remember why she'd stopped loving him.

Raylan's thumb brushed over the back of her hand, his touch as familiar as her own name. "I would have never let you go."

She scoffed, not because she didn't believe him, but because his words awoke a hope in her chest that she thought she'd squashed the day she left Crooked Valley in her rearview mirror. "What, you'd have followed me to New York?"

"If that's what it took. I wish I had. I really do." His voice was tender, sweet, full of all the emotions both of them had tamped down for so long. They were the same feelings Mia was terrified to embrace again. "I've never met anyone else like you, Mia. And I doubt I ever will again."

For a second, nothing existed but this moment. The case, her grandfather, their argument about the interrogation—none of it mattered because she was seventeen all over again and falling head over heels for the captain of the football team. "Raylan—"

The sound of a branch cracking made both of them jump inside the cabin, scrambling to hide in the corner again. Raylan waved for her to get behind him at the same time he bent down to retrieve the pan and she picked up the table leg again. "Get down, Mia. He could be back."

Her heart thudded in her chest, and she bit back the urge to scream. She peered around Raylan's shoulder, bracing herself for the blast of a rifle, the inevitable end that would bring.

And then...

"Wait, Raylan." She put a hand on the cast-iron pan, lowering it before Raylan went charging into the woods. "I think that's my grandfather."

As she said the words, Grandpa Louis emerged from the woods, looking exhausted and older than he had this morning. Leaves covered his sweater, mud streaked across his sneakers and he was breathing hard. The cane that he normally used had been replaced by a thick branch.

She climbed out of their hiding place and headed toward him. "Grandpa! What are you doing here?"

Relief broke over his face. "Mia! Thank God you're okay!"

Raylan came up beside her. Mia saw the exact moment Raylan switched into ADA mode. The softness in him disappeared and he strode toward Grandpa Louis with purpose. "Ironic that you are here right now, Mr. Beaumont. The person who shot at us ran into the woods right about where you are standing. It's a pretty strange coincidence that you just randomly came out of those very same woods."

"I heard the gunfire and was so worried someone might be shooting at the two of you." He hobbled closer to her. "Are you sure you're okay, Mia?"

"I'm fine, Grandpa. I'm more worried about you." She slipped an arm around his waist and helped him sit down on a makeshift bench created out of a log and a couple stumps. Grandpa let out a heavy sigh when he sat down, and Mia's worry multiplied. He looked and sounded exhausted. "Why are you driving around by yourself? And more, why are you traipsing through the woods?"

"I figured if no one else was going to find out what happened to Richard, I'd have to take matters into my own hands. I felt good today and decided to search the property. I saw your car, and a car I didn't recognize, but I didn't see you. I got worried, especially when I didn't see you in the house or anywhere nearby. I didn't know if someone took you or what happened, so I called the police and then I headed into the woods, trying to find you." He brushed a tendril of hair off her forehead in typical Grandpa fashion. He was more concerned about her than he was about himself. "Are you really sure you're okay? I couldn't bear it if something happened to you because of all this foolishness."

"Yes, I'm totally okay." The sound of the sirens grew closer and a moment later, Mia could see the flashing lights far in the distance as the cops drove up Harrington's driveway. The trees in this area of the woods parted just enough for anyone to get a clear view of the mansion. Raylan had been right. The shooter had been lying in wait here, watching them. The thought chilled her and made her want to get her grandfather as far away from this place as possible. "The police are here. Maybe one of the officers should follow you home, Grandpa. Make sure you get there safely."

"Not without me asking you a few questions first, Mr. Beaumont." Raylan took a step closer to Grandpa.

"What on earth could you be interrogating him for this time?" Mia shot to her feet. "For being in the wrong place at the right time? For all we know, Grandpa scared off the shooter."

"Or the shooting stopped because he is involved with the shooter." Raylan cast an accusatory look at Louis. "Are you involved, Mr. Beaumont?"

"You think that stick he's using for a cane is some kind of lethal weapon, Raylan? Or that my grandfather is a part of this because he was so worried he came looking for me in the middle of these woods?" She shook her head and rose on her toes to look him directly in his eyes. All those emotions she'd been feeling a moment ago had disappeared, replaced with hurt and disappointment. "All you ever see is guilt when you look at other people. Maybe it's time you start looking for innocence instead."

Raylan had spent hours going through the files in his office, looking for all the various pieces and parts of the Harrington case that his disorganized father had put in all kinds of different locations. No wonder Susan had always seemed frustrated working for his father. The first thing Raylan intended to do after the Harrington case was closed was organize this place.

Doing that had been a lot easier than dealing with the regrets he had about how he'd handled the shooting in the woods or how he kept undermining his relationship with Mia. They'd had a moment there, a moment that had allowed hope to grow in his heart, and then he'd ruined it all by basically accusing her elderly grandfather of being the shooter.

Raylan knew it was physically impossible for Louis Beaumont to chase after them with a rifle. It was also pretty unlikely that Mia's grandfather would hire someone to threaten her life, even if she was getting close to the truth. After all, her grandfather had been the one to ask her to solve the mystery. He wouldn't have done that if he wanted her to unmask him as a killer. Would he?

Raylan had seen less believable things over the years. Husbands who called the police on themselves after killing their wives. A daughter who tried to run over her own father with the car, and the father had tried to cover up the crime as an accident. When it came to family, people could get desperate.

But he'd seen Louis Beaumont with Mia dozens of times when they were younger. Unless Raylan's radar was completely off, Louis didn't seem like the kind of man who exacted revenge or planned shootings. He'd had that moment in the interrogation where he admitted to being greedy, but was that enough to consider as a motive?

All Raylan knew was that he needed more answers before he could ask the right questions.

Raylan spent the remains of his weekend and most of Monday looking through the files, trying to find answers to the dozens of questions in his mind. Why would someone be so intent on driving Raylan and Mia away from the Harrington house? Raylan didn't believe it was a scared squatter, as the Crooked Valley police seemed to think. There had to be a connection to the Harrington case. There just had to be.

Focusing on that also kept him from thinking too much about Mia. About what she was doing and whether she was safe. If the shooter would get desperate enough to come into town and go after Mia or Raylan in person. He'd texted Mia over the weekend, but her answers had been short and distant. He couldn't blame her for being angry at his mistrust of her grandfather. He'd feel the exact same way if someone accused one of his family members of such a crime. It was entirely possible that Louis Beaumont was as innocent as all the others who had lost their money the day Harrington disappeared.

Except…there was still something about this case that nagged at the back of Raylan's mind. Two bodies on Harrington's property, both killed around the same time Harrington disappeared. Millions of missing dollars. And a suspect who wanted to scare away anyone who got too close.

Could the shooter be Harrington himself? Or

was Raylan chasing after shadows that weren't really there?

There was a knock on the door, and Raylan looked up from the pile of papers before him. Hugh, his boss, stood in the doorway. The district attorney was a man who loved hiking in his spare time and who often came to work straight from a morning climb. He'd been a good district attorney, fair and earnest, and Raylan liked working for him. "Find anything?"

Raylan shook his head. "I've spent most of my time trying to figure out my father's filing system. His notes are everywhere except for where they should be."

"Have fun with that. Your father was a great attorney, but not the most organized person in this office. I wonder…" Hugh shook his head.

"Wonder what?"

"If your father's growing disorganization was a sign of the Alzheimer's he now has. If it was, I'm sorry I didn't see it when I was sitting in your chair."

Raylan gave Hugh a sympathetic smile. "None of us saw it coming, Hugh. It's not your fault."

Hugh nodded, but it was clear both of them felt guilt about not realizing Frank Westfield was declining as quickly as he did. It was almost a blessing that Raylan's mother hadn't been here to see it, because losing her husband and the wonderful memories they'd had would have broken her heart. Raylan knew his father was safe and well-cared for in the memory care unit where he lived, but he sure wished he could talk to his father about this case and share one more investigation story with him.

Maybe that was part of what had made Raylan so dedicated to his work, and also gun-shy about getting married. He'd lost his mother and lost the essence of his father. The people he loved most in the world had left his life sooner than they should have, leaving Raylan with a gaping hole in his heart and a fear of getting close to anyone again. Yet, where had that gotten him? The only woman he'd ever truly loved lived clear across the country, and he lived here alone, working himself to death.

Now he had very likely torched that relationship by stubbornly accusing her grandfather of crimes he probably didn't commit. Self-destruction at its finest.

Hugh took a seat in the visitor's chair and crossed one leg over the opposite knee. "What's your read on Beaumont? Do you think he had anything to do with it?"

"I don't think so. He lost everything when Harrington disappeared." Raylan opened the folder he'd unearthed in the back of one of the cabinets—it had been nestled between two completely different cases that weren't even alphabetically arranged—and turned it so the DA could read the columns on the right page. "Their firm had millions in investments. Beaumont invested everything he had saved—close to a million dollars—three months before Harrington disappeared."

"Isn't that why he claimed he didn't do it? Because he lost his savings, too?"

"He did, and everything I've seen in his finances over the last thirty years says he's speaking the truth."

Hugh shrugged. "Harrington could have just not told him where the money was."

"It's possible. But I think Harrington was in more trouble than we realized. When I took a closer look at the books, I saw that the upward trajectory of Harrington's investing took a sudden downturn just a week or so before he went missing."

"I think I remember hearing that about the case." Hugh nodded. "But that could also point to a motive for Beaumont. He was so upset that Harrington lost his savings that he reacted without thinking."

Raylan had considered the same thing. Maybe Louis had acted out of anger and killed Harrington because his business partner had been hemorrhaging money. Still, there had been millions in the company accounts, and a loss of several hundred thousand dollars out of Louis's investments would have been extremely upsetting and a possible motive for murder, but...

There was something that Raylan was missing, some key that would tie this all together, but what it was, he didn't know. "I also found an old letter from the SEC. Apparently they were investigating Richard Harrington for securities fraud."

"Wow." Hugh took the letter from Raylan and

scanned the text. "Do you think Beaumont killed Harrington to cover this up?"

"I don't know. From what I can tell, the SEC dropped the investigation after the investor *and* the investment disappeared. They probably figured they'd reopen it when Crooked Valley PD found Harrington, but that never happened. I'll make some calls tomorrow and follow up either way. That's not all." Raylan pointed to a time stamp on another document. "Most of the money was withdrawn that morning, but Harrington had withdrawn a hundred thousand a few days before he disappeared."

"Maybe a test run?"

"Maybe. Or maybe he was trying to pay someone off. That's a lot of money to withdraw at once. I don't see any kind of purchase, like a car or a boat, in his records." Raylan leaned back in his chair and voiced the suspicion that had been growing in his head the more he dug into this case and thought about the likely outcomes. "Frankly, Hugh, I don't think Richard Harrington ever left Colorado. But his money probably did. That clears Beaumont, in my mind."

Hugh shook his head. "To me, that makes Louis Beaumont look *more* like a suspect, because if he found out that Richard took all the firm's money, he had enough motive to kill him. But if Beaumont knew about the money possibly being transferred somewhere else, then where is it now?"

That was the question Raylan didn't have an answer to. Beaumont had lived like a pauper for several years, working his tail off to support his family. A man with millions of dollars surely wouldn't do that, would he? Maybe he would if the eye of suspicion had hung over him for three decades. Or maybe Harrington never told Beaumont where the money was and the old man had been searching for treasure when he was in the woods, not his granddaughter. "I think that's an answer everyone wants right now."

"Once you get it, you should take the reins on prosecuting this one. You're doing a great job, Raylan." Hugh got to his feet. "Good enough to be the next DA, for sure."

That was what Raylan had been working toward all his life. Filling his father's shoes and continuing the family legacy. But for some reason, this time the idea of putting together a case that would throw the bad guy in jail—especially if that bad guy was Louis Beaumont—didn't sit well with Raylan's soul.

Mia lingered at the counter of Three Sisters Grindhouse, nursing a coffee that had gone cold long ago. Every time she was in the coffee house, another childhood memory returned. Mia could remember her mother hoisting her onto a wooden barstool, then teaching her how to brew a perfect cup of coffee. From the second the girls had been old enough to hold a spoon, they had been in the back, helping to bake the cookies and sprinkle blueberries into the glistening muffin batter. Being here made her feel closer to her late grandmother. It was a nice feeling.

Mia dropped her gaze back to the work in front of her. She'd spent all of Monday researching, chatting with her grandfather and writing out a long list of the clues she had so far. In all those hours, she'd come up with...nothing. But it had kept her from dwelling on Raylan and the confusing jumble of emotions she was feeling for him. This would all be much better once she was back in New York and far from reminders of a love that was in the past. Or should be, given how her heart had reacted to him protecting her.

Then he'd gone and practically proclaimed her grandfather a murderer, reminding Mia that the two of them weren't on the same team and never had been. The only way to protect her grandfather was to find out what really happened to Richard Harrington.

She'd headed to the coffee shop in the late afternoon, hoping the change of location would spark some ideas. Mia flipped through her notes, rereading everything she had for the hundredth time.

Chloe slipped onto the stool beside her sister. "How's it going?"

"Not so good. I'm missing something, but I don't know what it is." Mia sighed. "If I don't figure this out, Grandpa is going to get arrested." She told her sister about the cabin and her grandfather's appearance in the woods and Raylan's reaction. Mia had stayed up most of the night last night worrying about whether the police department would show up and drag her grandfather in again. Raylan had texted a few times over the last couple days to check on her, but she'd brushed him off and asked about the case. All he'd told her was that he was still investigating, but that didn't give her any indication of which way the ADA was leaning. "It looks really bad for Grandpa Louis."

"Surely they don't think he was shooting at you?" Chloe said.

"No, but they think he paid someone, or at least that's what I overheard the cops saying just before we left the cabin. I've got to show them that isn't the case, but how do I prove that Grandpa *didn't* do something? Especially with a crime that happened thirty years ago?" Mia gestured at all the folders and notebooks in front of her. None of them provided a rock-solid alibi or an answer that would point far, far away from Grandpa as a suspect. "That's so much more difficult than proving someone did do something."

"I've seen your show. You're really good at this. If anyone has what it takes to prove Grandpa's innocence, it's you."

Mia sighed again and shuffled the papers around to start from the beginning again. Her sister's support gave her a little flicker of hope. Maybe Chloe had a point. "I hope you're right."

"So how's Raylan?" Chloe took Mia's mug, dumped it out and refilled it with fresh, hot coffee.

"He's a distraction I don't need." Mia put her chin in her hands and admitted a few hard truths to herself. For all her frustration with Raylan's insistence that Grandpa had something to do with Harrington's disappearance, he had also run after a shooter with no more protection than a pan. Just to make sure she was safe. That had touched a part of her heart she thought she'd closed off to him years ago. "That's not exactly true. Even though he's looking at this from the opposite angle as me, he's had some good ideas and, in a weird way, understands what I'm trying to do. He's also just doing his job, and I have to respect that."

"Well, that's good. It's always helpful to have someone to lean on when you're going through a stressful time. That's what I love about Bob. There's nothing more stressful than a new baby and—"

"What did you say?"

"There's nothing more stressful than a new baby?"

"No. Before that." Mia leaned forward, the coffee forgotten. "About having someone to lean on."

Chloe picked up a dish towel and started drying the freshly washed mugs. "Oh, I was just saying that Bob has been a great support. He's changing diapers and—"

"Sorry, sis, but I have to go." Mia gathered all her papers into a pile and stuffed them into her tote bag. She was halfway to the door before she turned back. "I'm glad you have Bob. And I look forward to getting to know him better once this case is solved."

Chloe studied her sister and grinned. "Wait…does that mean you're planning on staying in Crooked Valley?"

Mia shook her head. "It means I'm planning on being a better sister than I have been up till now." She dashed behind the counter and gave Chloe a quick hug. "Now I really have to go."

"Where are you going?"

"To see Raylan and tell him about how everyone needs someone they can lean on. Especially when they're afraid." Just as she had in that cabin a few days ago.

Chapter Eight

Mia headed out to her car and had almost made it to the CR-V when a short, bespectacled reporter rushed up to her, a microphone in his hand that was headed toward her face. He was underdressed for the weather, which meant he was either a local who had long ago grown used to the cold or an out-of-towner who'd underestimated the Crooked Valley winters. "Ms. Beaumont, what do you think about your grandfather's involvement in Richard Harrington's disappearance?"

"No comment."

"Really? You're not going to give a fellow journalist anything?" The guy's young face was earnest and eager, the way Mia herself had been when she first launched her YouTube channel, so desperate to make a difference in the world. She softened her stance. A little.

"Depends on whether you're looking for a headline or the truth," Mia said.

"Truth." The young man lowered his microphone and met her gaze. "I promise. I work for a local paper, and all I've ever tried to do is get to the truth."

"Now *that* I can appreciate." Mia motioned toward a bench on the sidewalk. "I only have a couple minutes, but I'll give you a few quotes." The two of them sat down, and true to her word, Mia gave the journalist, who turned out to be right around Mia's age, her own take on the case. At the end, the reporter handed her his card. Eddie Carter, freelance writer. She pocketed it and then reached out to shake his hand. "Thanks, Eddie. Just be sure you do right by my grandfather. He's had enough bad press that he didn't deserve or ask for."

"All I'm looking for is the truth. Just like you." Eddie waved goodbye and climbed into his car.

Mia prayed that was the case. If the DA did bring charges against Grandpa Louis, as he'd hinted at possibly doing in that impromptu press conference, it would help to have the media on her grandfather's side. The court of public opinion could be very, very powerful. Hopefully, powerful enough to overrule anything the DA said. If she could get Raylan to see how unrealistic it was for her grandfather to be some mastermind criminal, then maybe Raylan could convince the DA to stop going down this foolish path.

She pulled out of the lot and was halfway to Raylan's office when she realized going to him with that kind of argument might be a mistake. All trusting

Raylan had done was get her grandfather dragged in for questioning and reconsidered as a suspect, a fact the interview with Eddie had driven home. The more information she gave to Raylan, the more information she was possibly feeding to law enforcement. She was a fool to think Raylan would be on her side.

Raylan was, as Mia herself had said, just doing his job. She could respect that, but not be an idiot who put Grandpa Louis at risk of becoming indicted, too. She couldn't trust Raylan, not until she had enough information to prove, beyond a shadow of a doubt, that he was looking at the wrong suspect.

She also had to wonder if she was rushing to Raylan's office simply because she'd had a few tender thoughts about him. Missing him wasn't the best foundation for any kind of decision like that, especially when her grandfather's life was at stake.

Mia did a U-turn at the next intersection and drove toward her grandfather's house instead. His dependable Cutlass sat in the driveway, coated with a fine layer of snow. The air was crisp, forecasting an incoming storm. That was one thing she had missed about Crooked Valley—the beautiful winter storms that whistled down the mountains and changed every inch of the landscape in a matter of hours. Out here, she could breathe, think and simply be. She wondered vaguely if the hiking trails she had loved as a kid were still open. And if she'd stay in town long enough to enjoy them again. Right now, the city of New York seemed very, very far away.

Later, when Grandpa was safe and the mystery was solved, she could wonder about snowstorms and spring hikes. She grabbed her tote bag and hurried into the house. The kitchen was empty, although a teakettle was simmering on the stove. "Hey, Grandpa, where are you?"

"In here. Taking it easy, as ordered by Doctor Mia."

She laughed as she came into the living room and saw that he was, indeed, tucked into his favorite chair, a blanket draped over his legs. The television was playing an old black-and-white movie that she had seen her grandfather watch several times before with her grandmother. He had a stack of books and an odd-looking small statue of some kind sitting on the end table beside him. He looked cozy, comfortable and far less exhausted than he had a few days ago, which made Mia relieved. "I'm glad to see you doing better."

"I shouldn't have gone out to the property. I don't know what I was thinking." He shook his head. "I'm not as young as I once was."

"Even though going into the woods to look for me was foolish and very brave, I'm glad you did because it's very likely that you being there scared away the shooter." Mia covered her grandfather's hand with her own. "But you have to promise me you won't do anything like that again."

"I'm just so frustrated. The police still think I

had something to do with Richard's disappearance. I don't know how to make them see reason."

Mia had been struggling with the same thoughts, but didn't tell her grandfather that. He was worrying more than enough for both of them right now, and the last thing she wanted to do was take away his hope that she could solve this thing. That task seemed impossible, but with Chloe, Julia and Grandpa rooting for her, Mia had to try to look down at least one more avenue for clues.

"I think the only way to do that is to show them another possibility." Mia dug in her bag and took out her notepad and a pen before she took a seat on the sofa. "Something Chloe said to me today got me thinking."

"I'm glad you girls are spending time together. It's been lovely to have us all together again."

"I agree." Mia twisted the pen back and forth. "I hadn't realized how much I missed them until I came back home. Even if it may be too late to have a relationship."

Her grandfather waved that off with his typical disbelief that there could ever be any strife between the Beaumont girls. "Pshaw. Your sisters love you and have missed you, too."

"Chloe, yes. Julia… I'm not so sure." Despite seeing her sister a few times since Mia returned, most of their interactions had been stiff and unemotional. Part of that was all the years that Mia had stayed away, she was sure, but it was also more hurtful than

Mia had expected. When she was a little girl, she'd been closest to Julia, but as the girls became teenagers and dovetailed down their own individual paths, that closeness ebbed away.

"You know your older sister," Grandpa said as the teakettle began to whistle. He got to his feet, putting a hand up to stop Mia from getting the tea. He headed into the kitchen and kept talking as he poured them each a mug of decaf green tea. "She keeps her emotions close to her chest."

Mia scoffed. "All of them except annoyance."

"That's not annoyance, granddaughter." Grandpa put her cup of tea on the table beside the small sofa. The fruity blend wafted up a sweet scent. "It's hurt."

"What does Julia have to be hurt about?" Mia cupped her hands around the warm mug and took a tentative sip. The tea was hot and perfect for a cold night in the valley.

"She was devastated when you left Crooked Valley." Grandpa dunked his bag over and over again, the way her grandmother used to do it. "You and she are only a year apart, and when you were little, you two were thick as thieves. She missed having you here."

"She's never said anything like that to me."

"Julia's the oldest, the one who stepped in as the adult when your mother worked so much." Finally satisfied with the tea, he took a sip and then smiled at Mia over the brim of the cup. "Maybe that's kept her from acting like she needed you, too."

"Because we were so busy needing her." Mia thought about that for a long moment. She remembered leaning on her older sister so many times when they were young. And every time, Julia had been there, in one way or another. "You might have a point, Grandpa. But either way, I'm too focused on the investigation to worry about family issues."

Grandpa Louis covered her hand with his own. "The only thing that matters, my dear granddaughter, is family. Everything else is ephemeral."

Not if you end up in prison. That's a very real and tangible possibility, and then my family is broken forever, and that's an outcome I can't handle.

Mia sighed. One family matter at a time. Once Grandpa's future was secure, Mia could work on her relationship with Julia. So she changed the subject. "What's that statue you have there?" She gestured toward the table.

"Oh, this?" Her grandfather picked up the small bronze item and turned it over in his hand. "This is one half of a set of bookends that Richard bought when we first opened the company. They're buffalo, which used to roam the expanses of Colorado back in the day."

Mia thought back to the little bit of Native American history that she remembered. "Buffalos are a symbol of abundance, right?"

Her grandfather nodded. "He bought a pair of these—kept one for himself and gave me the other. But there's more to these bookends than just how they sit on a shelf." He turned it over and pointed out a circle on the bottom. "They have a compartment inside. Richard said we should put something that represented the future we dreamed of in here, sort of like a reverse time capsule."

"What did you put in yours?"

He turned the dial and a cylinder popped out. Inside was a hundred-dollar bill. "This was the first investment we ever received, from a widow who lived out on Red Canyon Road. I wanted to always remember where we started at, so I kept it in here. I invested my own hundred dollars for her, of course, but kept the cash she gave me as a reminder. No matter how bleak things got after Richard left, I kept this bill in here. I guess I hoped that if I did, someday things would go back to where they were when we were young and excited, and it seemed like the opportunities for success were endless."

Her heart broke for her optimistic grandfather, who had put everything he had into a company and a business partner who eventually let him down. For the first time since beginning this investigation, Mia felt anger and hatred toward Richard for doing this to her sweet, trusting grandfather. "What did Richard put inside his?"

"You know, I never asked." Her grandfather stared at the bookend a while longer, then replaced it on the end table. "I don't remember seeing his at the office when I closed the doors, so he must have kept his at home."

Mia jotted down a note reminding her to look for the buffalo the next time she was in the Harrington house. The chances of it being any kind of clue to Harrington's disappearance were zero, but at this point, she was willing to try anything. "While we're talking about the case, I wanted to ask you a few more questions about Richard, if you have time."

"At my age, all I have is time on my hands." He smiled wistfully. "I never thought I'd say it at the time, but I miss those days when I was so busy being a husband and father. I remember Richard telling me once that I was the most blessed man alive because I had all those girls in my life."

All those girls who were now gone. Grandma had passed on, Mom and Mia had moved away, and Chloe and Julia were busy with families of their own. It had to be tough for Grandpa to be alone, especially with so much at stake. Most people leaned on the ones closest to them when they were caught in a stressful situation. Maybe Richard Harrington had done the same.

"Did Richard have a special girl in his life? I know he never married, but did he have a girlfriend?"

Grandpa cupped his chin and thought back. "You know, I don't remember if he did or not. Richard was always fairly private. Almost…reclusive. And to be honest, your grandmother and I had our hands full with three little girls, so I can't say I paid attention to Richard's personal life. Why do you ask?"

"I just thought I could track her down and see if she has any memories from around that time."

Grandpa Louis took another sip of tea. "Well, surely if he was dating someone, her name would be in the police report."

"Maybe. But since the case was never closed, I only got redacted pages." She'd been all over those documents today and hadn't seen a mention of a girl-friend or wife. There was so much that was blacked out, however, and one of those sections could contain the clue she needed. "I can't see everything that's in the file."

As Mia reached for her teacup, she realized she knew one person who could. The question was whether it was worth the price she'd have to pay to ask him for help.

Raylan picked up the phone and leaned back in his office chair. It had taken several transfers and a lot of time on hold, but Morales had finally tracked down someone in the US Securities and Exchange Commission office who had information about the Harrington investigation.

"The agent I reached knew the one who had spent some time looking into that case," the detective told Raylan. "He was sure that Harrington, and maybe Beaumont, were up to no good but couldn't prove it because it wasn't just the money that disappeared.

It was the books, too. Back in those days, they kept their accounting in general ledgers. Computers were a fairly new thing."

The books, too? That meant someone had something to hide, some nefarious transactions. Had that someone been Harrington? Or Mia's grandfather? "What's your gut telling you on this?"

"I don't know. This is the kind of thing that could go either way. Maybe Harrington was trying to cover his tracks before he disappeared, or maybe he discovered Beaumont was embezzling and Beaumont killed him."

"Except none of that money is in Beaumont's accounts. He doesn't have a house in Barbados or a fifty-foot yacht he can't explain buying. If he was embezzling, then he'd have money to show for it."

Morales let out a long sigh. "I agree with you, but I'm still going to get a warrant to look at Beaumont's business books. I don't know if they'll go back that far, but it's worth a shot."

"Keep me posted." Raylan hung up the phone and then buzzed Susan. "Did you find anything else in my father's files?"

"No, Raylan. I'm sorry. I think you have everything there is on the case."

He thanked her and bit back his frustration. Susan had gone above and beyond helping him reorganize the bulk of his father's files when he'd first started as ADA. She had done a great job in the office, but the materials his father had taken home had been left in cubbies and corners of the house. Even though Raylan had corralled and stored everything he'd found in bank boxes when he cleaned out Dad's house after he moved into the memory care unit, there was always a chance that Dad had left some crucial piece of evidence in a sock drawer or something.

His father had been a brilliant prosecutor who didn't care about organization because he had a pinpoint memory for details, but as that memory began to fail him, the disorganization became worse, as if Frank couldn't hold on to any of the details that mattered. It was only a year or so later that his father had been forced to retire and eventually move into assisted living and then memory care. Raylan wished his father was here today to discuss this case and so many other things.

Like the confusing feelings Raylan still had for Mia. He'd thought he'd forgotten her after she left. He'd dated several other women, considered marrying one of them, but Mia being back here in person showed him why it had never worked out with anyone else.

Because no other woman was as captivating—and as infuriating—as Mia Beaumont. She was smart but stubborn. Compassionate but confusing. He'd thought he'd seen something in her eyes that day in the woods, something that had made him wonder if maybe, just maybe, no one else had ever captured her heart, either.

He heard a knock on his door and glanced up to

see Susan standing in the doorway with Mia, as if he'd conjured her up merely by thinking about her. "Oh, hi. What—what are you doing here?"

"Mia wanted to talk about the case," Susan answered before Mia could. "But I was thinking that it's lunchtime and you didn't bring a lunch, Raylan, and Mia is surely starving, so maybe you two should grab a bite to eat while you talk."

"Susan, I—"

"You have such a busy schedule today, Raylan. Doesn't it make sense to have an extra meeting over lunch?" Susan gave him a not-so-innocent, who-me matchmaking smile.

Mia put up a hand. "Raylan, we don't have to meet today. I'm sorry. I was just being impatient."

"No, no, it's fine." He was flustered, caught in the memory of her smile and his own increasingly complicated feelings about her, while also trying to act professional. "You and I both want to get this case closed, and I don't think we should procrastinate on that."

"Great. So lunch it is." Susan bustled into Raylan's office and handed him his coat before he could protest. Then she ushered the two of them through the office and out onto the sidewalk, talking the entire time, preventing them from getting a word in edgewise.

"I have to apologize for Susan," Raylan said after she had waved at them and then returned back inside. "She has it in her mind that we…well, we…"

"Should get back together. That would be a terrible idea."

"Yes, terrible." He slipped a sideways glance at her. But Mia's face was unreadable.

"We don't have to get lunch. I really just had one or two quick things I wanted to run past you."

He could keep playing this game of hiding his feelings, or he could be up-front and honest for once. When he was a teenager, he'd pretended it didn't shatter his heart when they broke up, and look where that had got him—alone and missing her for more than a decade. Maybe it was time to be a whole lot more truthful about how he felt.

"Actually, I'd love to get lunch with you. It's been nice having you back in Crooked Valley, Mia, and I'd like to spend more time with you."

Her mouth opened. Closed. "Oh, well, yes. I, uh, think that's a great idea. We have the case to work on and…"

He stopped on the sidewalk and met her gaze. "I don't want to talk about the case."

"You don't? But you just said we shouldn't procrastinate."

"And we won't. I have a meeting in an hour, so, for the next—" he glanced at his watch "—forty-five minutes, I want to just talk to you, like we used to. When we walk back to my office, we can talk about the case. How does that sound?"

"Honestly? Terrifying." She let out a little laugh.

"It sounds a lot like a date, and to be honest, it's been a long time since I've had one of those."

"Me, too. You might have to remind me all over again how to keep a girl's interest."

"You don't need any lessons in that," Mia said softly. She spun away and started walking again before he could press her for more. "So, uh, lunch. What are we eating?"

Retreating to the safer ground of choosing a restaurant gave Raylan a moment to process what Mia had just said. He'd learned two things that, right now, were much more interesting than any case he'd ever worked on: Mia hadn't dated anyone in a long time, and she was just as distracted by him as he was by her.

That news made his steps a little lighter and the stress of the day disappear. He felt like a teenager again, overwhelmed by the rush he got every time he was near her.

They talked through several food options but eventually settled on returning to Cappy's Diner. "What does it say about us that we end up at the same place over and over again? Even after all these years?"

"That maybe the past wasn't as bad as we thought."

"Maybe it wasn't." A small smile crossed her lips.

Cappy welcomed them just as warmly the second time, but with a knowing grin. "Always nice to see you two, especially when you're together."

Two weeks ago, that would have been a cringeworthy statement, but after spending all this time with Mia, both investigating and…well, running for their lives, he realized how nice it was to have her by his side. She blushed at Cappy's comment but didn't brush it off.

They ordered the burgers again, and it felt comfortable and perfect. As they settled in with their drinks and a basket of fries they'd decided to split, Mia was the first to speak. "So, Raylan, what have you been up to since I left town?" She blushed again. "Sorry. I'm horrible at small talk."

He chuckled. "Me, too, so don't feel bad. What have I been up to? Pretty much what you see right now. My father retired because of his memory issues and now lives in a memory care unit about a half hour from here. I never intended to follow in his footsteps. After I passed the bar, I had planned to go into defense work because it's so much more lucrative, but once he had to retire, I thought there was no better way to honor my father than to follow in his shoes."

"I am sure he's proud as a peacock."

"I'm not sure he even understands what I say when I visit him, but that's not why I do it. My father was an incredible prosecutor, and I want to be able to do even half as good a job as he did and help keep another generation of Crooked Valley safe."

"That is a very noble goal." She smiled at him, and his heart warmed. They exchanged a long look, and then Mia glanced away. "So, um…do you still play football?"

"I wish I had time to, but ever since I went to work for the district attorney's office, things have been hectic. Crime, unfortunately, doesn't have a season. It's year-round." He took a sip of his soda. "What about you? Do you still run?"

"As often as I can, though not as fast as I did in cross-country." She grinned and plopped a fry in her mouth.

"None of us are as fast as we were in high school, but to me, that's a good thing."

"Why do you say that?"

"Moving slower, even if it's only by a few minutes, gives you the opportunity to appreciate the world, look around at all the beauty here."

Her gaze followed his out the window to the mountain that shadowed most of Crooked Valley. "That's one thing I've missed. The hiking, the nature and just being in the wilderness here."

"You didn't get enough wilderness when we were being shot at in the woods?" He laughed and put up his hands. "Sorry. I know I said we wouldn't talk about the case at lunch."

"Ten-point deduction for you, Mr. Westfield." She wagged a fry in his direction.

"We're keeping score?"

"Always." She grinned and ate another fry. "I'd like to get in a hike or two before I go back to New York."

"Do you like it there?"

She shrugged. "I used to think I did, but now..." She glanced out the window again. "Crooked Valley has this kind of magic that nowhere else possesses."

"It does indeed," he agreed, but he wasn't looking at the landscape. He was looking at the graceful lines of Mia's face, the way her smile lit up her eyes and how everything about her felt like home.

When the burgers came, Mia was almost disappointed. Not by the food, but by the reminder that they were here for lunch and then work. This wasn't a date, and it wasn't a moment when she should be rekindling her relationship with Raylan. Although for a minute there, she had considered doing exactly that.

They ate and chatted in the same comfortable, warm way they had when they were younger. She realized that she really liked this adult version of Raylan. Liked him a lot. She found it endearing when he fiddled with his glasses. She liked that his hair was longer, but his smile was the same.

The check came, and even though Mia insisted they split it, Raylan slipped his credit card into the holder and handed it to the waitress before she could add her card. "Raylan, this wasn't a date." She said the words to remind herself as much as him.

"Of course it wasn't. Just two old friends catching up."

She should have been happy to hear him say that,

but the word *friends* stung more than she expected it to. She struggled to put a smile on her face as she slipped on her coat and followed him out into the cold.

As they did, Mia caught a glimpse of a figure in black ducking behind a building. She stopped short and grabbed Raylan's arm. "I think I just saw him."

"Who?"

"The shooter." She'd lowered her voice to a whisper even though they were across the street and out of earshot. "I think I saw the same guy once before in Harrington's driveway. Even if he's not the shooter, he's involved somehow. I think he's following us."

Raylan put his hand over hers. "Even if that was him and even if he is following us, we're safe here, in the middle of town. And we're safe together."

The flash of terror that had zipped up her spine a moment ago began to ebb. There was something about Raylan's presence—so strong and steady and comfortable—that had her believing his words. The sun was bright, the sidewalk was busy and there was hopefully no way anyone would take a shot at them under these conditions. They began to walk again, and as they moved farther from the spot where she'd seen the figure, the more she believed she'd been mistaken. It was winter in Colorado. Pretty much everyone around here had a hooded sweatshirt on.

"Let's talk about the case now." Maybe if she got back on familiar ground, she could erase the feeling of dread that hung stubbornly to the edge of her thoughts.

"Of course. What'd you want to ask me when you came in today?"

She pulled her notepad out of her tote bag and flipped to the page with the notes she'd made when she'd talked to her grandfather. "Did Richard Harrington have a girlfriend? I didn't find any record of him being married, but he could have had someone in his life. There's so much of the police report that's redacted that I couldn't really tell if there was one mentioned in there or not."

Raylan thought for a minute. "I think he did. I had forgotten about her until you mentioned it. I don't remember seeing a witness statement for her, but I'll check with Morales to see what they have in their files."

"Good, because I wondered if maybe he relied on his girlfriend and either told her about his plans to leave or—"

"Told her about the money," Raylan said, finishing with her. "That's motive right there."

"Exactly."

"I'll look into it and get back to you." They kept walking, dodging people on the sidewalk as snowflakes began to fall from the sky. Just a dusting of snow, enough to make the town winter-pretty.

At some point, Raylan had released her arm, and although they were close together as they walked, they were no longer touching, and it felt like he'd moved a million miles away emotionally. That was what she wanted, wasn't it? A no-strings, get-to-work, leave-these-memories-behind stay in Crooked Valley?

If that was so, why did she have this persistent feeling of…disappointment? Had she really thought that one lunch would have Raylan declare he'd always loved her, and they'd ride off into the sunset together? Not only was that impossible, but it was also impractical. Her life was clear across the country in a place that seemed so much grayer than Crooked Valley. And she didn't want to fall in love and settle down in this town.

Did she?

Raylan cleared his throat. "So I learned something else that I definitely shouldn't share with you because this is an active investigation."

"That I am also actively investigating."

"If I tell you, you have to promise not to ask your grandfather about it until I have more information."

Mia swallowed her alarm. Was this something else that would point at Grandpa Louis as a suspect? And why did the air between them seem to suddenly change? All that warmth and familiarity they'd had back in the diner had disappeared in the cold, harsh light of a criminal investigation. It almost made Mia wish she wasn't here to solve a crime. Almost. "I promise not to tell him for a day or two, to give you time to get the information. But if this is something that can hurt or help his case, my grandfather deserves to know about it."

"He already does know about this, and yet, he never mentioned it to the police." They had reached the door to Raylan's office, but he didn't go in yet. "Richard, and by extension the company he had with your grandfather, was being investigated by the SEC for fraud."

"My grandfather? Fraud? There's no way. He's the most honest person I know."

"Either he was in on some fishy deals or he was working with someone who was. I find it hard to believe he didn't know what was going on in his own business."

"Richard handled all of the investing. My grandfather was more client-facing because he had the personality for it. If Grandpa was in sales, then it's possible he wouldn't have been aware of everything that was going on with the books, especially if Richard didn't talk about it. From what I heard, Richard was a gruff, introverted man. My grandfather is the total opposite."

"I hope, for your grandfather's sake, that he wasn't involved in any fraud. But the pieces that are adding up aren't looking good for him. Be prepared for this to go badly, Mia."

"Not everyone you meet is a criminal, Raylan." Mia sighed. "Please try to see the good in my grandfather instead of looking for a reason to put him in prison."

"I'm doing my best, Mia. I really am." He nodded goodbye and turned to go back into his building. Mia stood in the cold on the sidewalk for a long time, a jumble of emotions and questions tumbling inside her.

Chapter Nine

Raylan emerged from his meeting with Morales with a handful of answers and more questions. The cops had searched the woods around the Harrington estate as well as the house one more time and found no evidence of the shooter besides a few spent cartridges. Raylan told Morales about what Mia had seen downtown, but the description was too vague to mean anything. Whoever it was, Morales said, was probably long gone, especially after all this police activity. "You found his hiding spot. He has nowhere to go now, so I'm sure he skipped town."

"I hope you're right."

"I'll have a patrol car keep an eye on your office and Mia's grandfather's house," Morales said. "Just don't go out to that property without letting me know, okay? I don't need you to be the cowboy rushing in to solve the case."

Raylan chuckled. "Okay, I promise."

The conversation sifted through the various bits of evidence that the team had uncovered, which wasn't much. Morales said there'd been a note about Harrington's girlfriend, a woman he had known for a year or so named Dolores Rouse. They'd broken up three months before his disappearance. After that, she'd lived in a nearby town and had stayed there after Harrington disappeared. She'd married someone else, had a child and lived a decent life with a nice house, a couple cars, regular vacations. Nothing extravagant. Nothing that would say she was in possession of millions of dollars. She'd lived a quiet, predictable life and, after the first interview with the police, had been cleared as a suspect.

"Still, I think we should question her," Raylan said. "I'll cancel my afternoon appointments and we can go there right now."

Morales shook his head. "Too late. She died a month ago. Heart attack."

"That's so sad." Raylan let out a long breath. "There's another dead end."

"With a thirty-year-old case, you're going to have a lot of them. Sorry. We'll keep digging."

Raylan thanked Morales and walked the detective to the door. For the rest of the afternoon, he worked on other cases, but his mind kept circling back to the information the detective had shared about Dolores. She didn't sound like a murderer, but then again, in Raylan's experience, most people he prosecuted looked like the man or woman next door. The kind the neighbors would say was "the last person we'd expect to do this kind of thing."

At five, Susan went home, but Raylan stayed in his office. He and Hugh chatted about the case for a few minutes. In Hugh's mind, the main suspect was still Louis Beaumont. "I don't need to look anywhere else," Hugh said before he left. "The killer has been living in this town for decades. Just find enough to put him behind bars."

Instead, Raylan spent some time running an internet search on Dolores. The information the police department had on her was minimal. They'd done one short interview with her, describing her as timid but nice. Cooperative. Not at all bitter about Richard. She'd been dismissed as a suspect right away.

The rest basically repeated what Morales had said. Dolores had lived in a modest house ten miles away from Crooked Valley, worked for more than twenty-five years at the insurance agency owned by the man she eventually married, had been a member of her church and won a blue ribbon three times at the county fair for her apple pies. It all seemed like normal, run-of-the-mill reports. Raylan skimmed a half-dozen newspaper articles that had contained her name, mostly short interviews about the blue ribbons, and one shortly after Harrington disappeared. The final article, buried in the search results, was from a small local paper, the kind that was delivered weekly and usually featured information about festivals and craft fairs. The short piece written about

Dolores was maybe a thousand words long. Raylan was just about to click away when a caption beneath a photograph grabbed his attention. *He was a man who had secrets*, Dolores had said. *And secrets never like to see the light of day.*

In the photograph, Dolores was sitting on her front porch, drinking a cup of coffee and looking out into the distance. She looked tired and beaten down by life, the kind of woman who had a perpetual frown and a slump in her shoulders. The majority of the article was a twenty-five-year anniversary recap of the Harrington mystery, featuring an interview with Dolores that dropped the word obsessed to describe her demeanor. As far as Raylan could tell, none of the national or daily papers had picked up the story, but maybe that was because there wasn't much of a story there. The most intriguing part of the article was in that caption, but there was nothing else to go on for clues.

Dolores talked about meeting Richard when he came in to get new car insurance and having a whirlwind relationship that swept her off her feet when she was in her late twenties. Then he'd disappeared and she told the reporter she'd had no idea he was planning on leaving town. Even though they had broken up months before, she said that she used to talk to Richard every few days: *He just stopped calling me. I figured we weren't friends any longer so I moved on and started dating someone else. That man ended up becoming my husband, and we had a very happy mar-*

riage and a wonderful son. Richard Harrington disappearing was the best thing that ever happened to me.

Clearly, she wasn't much of a fan of Harrington, either. Like Mia had said, Richard had a reputation for being abrupt and almost rude with most people. Raylan printed out the article and added it to his file about the Harrington case. It was probably nothing more than a waste of ink, but unlike his father, Raylan liked to be organized and keep track of every little tidbit in one place.

He milled around the empty office for a little while, debating whether to tell Mia about the article. He had already shared far more than he should have about the case and knew that if Hugh found out, he'd be furious. Hugh was convinced Beaumont was the suspect they'd been looking for, even if it was clear someone else had been the shooter. Beaumont definitely had motive and, three decades ago, the strength and wherewithal to do something. But neither of those facts made him guilty.

When Raylan was younger, Mia had been his sounding board for everything. Which car he bought after he got his license. Which colleges he applied to. He'd valued her input and common-sense approach to decision-making. Even in a case involving her own family, she'd been rational and methodical in her research. Her take on Dolores's interview could provide another perspective that this difficult case clearly needed. Raylan never talked to anyone outside of law enforcement during the investigation phase, but there was just something about Mia's earnest desire to help her grandfather that tugged at Raylan's heartstrings.

Okay, and she was beautiful, too, and had never fully left his mind, despite their breakup twelve years ago. The memory of Mia had haunted every date he'd ever had and teased his dreams on the long nights when he'd been tired and lonely.

The long and short of it was simple—he missed her. He always had.

Before he could think better of it, Raylan picked up his phone and sent her a text. Found out some info about the girlfriend.

She replied right away. Anything you can tell me?

He thought for a second. Can't share anything over text. How about we meet tomorrow out at the Harrington place?

Aren't you worried about the shooter coming back?

Raylan hesitated. Morales was convinced the shooter had moved on and was no longer a threat. He'd also told Raylan not to go out to the Harrington property without letting the detective know first. Well, Raylan would do that—tomorrow. Crooked Valley PD says there's no sign of him, and we should be okay if you wanted to do some more searching or film some material for your show.

Thank you! That's great! I appreciate it!

Her enthusiasm warmed him and made Raylan wish he had more news to share. Instead, he signed off with a short discussion about what time to meet. Long after their business had been concluded, Raylan stared at the screen on his phone. Good night, Mia, he texted. I hope you have a great evening.

There was a long pause, so long that Raylan stopped waiting for her reply and started heading for his apartment. A mile from home, the screen on his car dashboard lit up with an incoming text from Mia. Raylan pushed Play. "You, too, Raylan. Can't wait to see you tomorrow." Even though the voice came from the computer, Raylan was convinced he could hear Mia's sweet tones in every word.

The next morning dawned bright but brisk, as the winter storm that had moved in yesterday began to settle heavily over the valley. More snow was on the way, along with a temperature drop, which meant the meeting with Mia at the Harrington place would be short.

The whole thing was probably a waste of time, a chasing of shadows that didn't exist. What were the chances that Harrington's girlfriend had been telling the truth about Harrington having secrets? And that those "secrets" were about him hiding money? Not to mention the chances of Raylan and Mia finding that money after dozens of officers had combed the estate multiple times. And yet, every clue in this case seemed to circle right back to the mansion. What was Raylan missing?

He parked in front of the massive brick home and looked up at its imposing facade. What other secrets were hiding inside these walls? *Secrets never like to see the light of day.*

Mia pulled up beside him and got out of her car. She was bundled up in a waist-length white coat with a faux-fur-trimmed hood and a pair of sturdy black boots. She looked beautiful and strong, and his heart did a little flip. "So what'd you find out?"

It took a second for his brain to refocus on why she was here in the first place. The case, not a relationship that had ended a long time ago. Raylan caught Mia up on what little he knew about the girlfriend. "Unfortunately, she died a month ago so we can't interview her."

The same frustration he'd felt flashed across Mia's face, and Raylan almost laughed at how similar the two of them were. "How serious do you think she was about there being secrets?"

Raylan shrugged. "I don't know. It was an odd statement to me. There were a couple people interviewed over the years who said she was never the same after Harrington disappeared. She'd always been a little odd and eccentric, but after Harrington left she became even more so. I asked Morales to talk to her husband. The man didn't know much, but he did say Dolores always resented Harrington for leaving her behind, even though they'd been broken up when he left."

"Seems like a long time to hold a grudge. Maybe he owed her money, too?"

"Maybe so. Morales is digging deeper into the financial records today." Raylan didn't mention that Morales wasn't just looking into Harrington's and Dolores's records—he was also looking into Louis Beaumont's company's history. "I'll let you know what he finds out about Dolores."

"And meanwhile…we look for what exactly?" She did a slow circle, her gaze taking in the vast, snow-dusted grounds. "The cops have searched this estate several times. What are we going to find that they didn't?"

"Dolores said, 'Secrets never like to see the light of day.'"

"That's an odd way to phrase it. Do you think it's a clue?"

"I don't know. I do know that Richard was paranoid about being robbed, especially because his house is rather remote." Raylan tapped a foot against the frozen earth.

"Ironic, given that he stole so many people's life savings." She thought for a second. "You mentioned the newspaper article was from a local paper. Was the reporter Eddie Carter by any chance?"

Raylan thought back. "Yes, I think so. Why?"

"He interviewed me yesterday." She must have seen the look on Raylan's face because she waved off his concerns. "Don't worry. I didn't tell him anything that would affect the case. It seems he's one of those reporters who wants to solve this as much as we do."

"Well, if his interview with Dolores proves to be the final clue we needed, I'll give him an exclusive interview. What Dolores said made me wonder if there was something buried here. Just because I thought it wouldn't hurt to be thorough, I went through the building plans, but there's nothing that shows any kind of structure beneath the house, other than your standard basement, and none of the investigators found anything when they were here. But then I thought about that body buried in the wall. If Harrington killed his assistant and her husband, and used the house to hide his crimes…"

"The house might still be hiding more crimes." She ducked back in her car and grabbed two heavy-duty flashlights. "All right. Let's get searching."

Raylan chuckled as he took one of the flashlights and led the way into the house. "That's what I like about you, Mia. You're adventurous."

"Julia would call it foolhardy."

"But your doggedness and the risks you took got an innocent man freed. Solved a forty-year-old murder. Brought closure to several families." He'd seen the teary, heartfelt testimonies on YouTube and read the many glowing articles about Mia Beaumont's undying quest for truth and justice. The two of them had so much in common in that, Raylan realized. If they hadn't been on opposite sides with this crime, they would have made an incredible team.

She grinned. "You *have* been watching my channel."

"I have. I like seeing this version of you. You've always been smart and talented, but what you do on that channel is on par with the best of detectives."

She dipped her head as if the compliment made her shy. "Well, thank you." They made their way down the hall and through the great room, with its twenty-five-foot ceiling and thick Oriental carpet. They entered the kitchen, then opened a door that led to the cellar. Out of habit, Mia flicked on the lights. "Whoops. I forgot the electricity was off."

"It's sad, really, that such a beautiful property has just been left to rot for three decades."

"Maybe someone will buy it from the city and give it the love it deserves." She hung back, allowing Raylan to go down the stairs first. He swung his flashlight as he walked, the two of them looking for clues and checking for any signs of the shooter.

"Looks like the shooter is long gone," Raylan said. "Maybe Morales was right and it was just a drifter."

"An armed drifter? Seems unlikely."

"I've seen stranger things in this world." Raylan stopped beside one of the concrete block walls that stretched the full length of the basement. "Well, the building plans were correct. There's nothing else here. No hidden tunnels or secret rooms."

"Life is not a Nancy Drew novel." She grinned. "Maybe we need to knock on the walls?"

"Well, that worked in the closet." He chuckled and then shrugged. "Let's try it." They spent the next half hour circling the space, rapping on the walls. But none of them sounded any different from the one before, and as far as Raylan could tell, there was nothing hollow behind any of the thick concrete blocks.

Mia sighed and leaned against a set of shelves stuffed with boxes. "I think—" The set of shelves moved, letting out a long screech as it shifted against the concrete floor. Mia scrambled away and the shelf stopped.

"Well, well. I think we found one of those secrets that has been kept in the dark for a long time." He shone his flashlight down at the space where the shelf used to stand, revealing a door. And a lock.

A thrill ran through Mia when they found the tunnels. This was what she lived for when she investigated cold cases. The excitement of turning up something that everyone else had missed.

She could see why the cops wouldn't have noticed the shelving unit. From the outside, it looked like it was an ordinary set of shelves, just like the three behind it. The boxes were all labeled with the kinds of things most people had in their basements—old books, sports equipment, tools. There were boxes of unopened saws and drills on the shelf, as if Harrington wanted to look like someone who was handy but never actually did the work.

"Here, help me move this." Raylan grabbed onto the unit.

The two of them got on one end and tugged the

unit to the right. It screeched and groaned the whole way, the mechanisms clearly affected by years of non-use. The unit moved another couple feet and then stopped, leaving an opening just big enough for someone to slip through.

"The entrance is locked." Raylan glanced around the cellar. "Let me see if I can find something to pry it open." He crossed to the other shelves and started going through boxes and bins.

Mia got out her phone and videotaped the shelves and the hole, then swung her flashlight past the boxes on the shelves in front of her. Something glinted in the dark, and she moved the light back. Something covered with dust and very, very familiar looking. She took a picture of it, then tucked her phone away. "I think I found the key."

Raylan came over to stand beside her. "What is that? A bookend?"

"Yes. My grandfather has one just like it. Richard said they should store something inside these for the future. If Richard was hiding the money in these tunnels, then I think the key is inside this." She twisted the circular bottom to the right and then pulled out the tube inside. A brass key dropped into her palm.

"Well, I'll be." Raylan shook his head. "That's amazing."

She bent down and inserted the key into the padlock, and a moment later, the lock sprung free. Mia wrestled it out of the metal ring while Raylan helped her lift the heavy trapdoor. They could see the top few steps of a metal ladder and not much else.

Mia shone her light past the ladder and into the hole, but it was so dark, the light was quickly swallowed. "Do you think we should go down there?"

"We should probably call Morales."

"Morales will want to search it himself," Mia countered. She could feel the excitement in the air, the possibilities that they might have just cracked a thirty-year-old mystery. The thought of solving it themselves—solving it together—overruled the common-sense idea of calling the police. "How about we just tell him we found it and then do a little snooping ourselves?"

He chuckled. "You're going to get me into trouble with the police chief."

"Not if we solve the Harrington mystery. Then you'll be a hero. And I'll have another cool show to put out." She grinned. "It's not all about you, Raylan."

"It was always all about you, Mia. At least for me," he said softly, then turned around and began going down the ladder, the flashlight clipped to his belt and illuminating a bouncing circle beneath him.

Mia took a second to process those words, the joy they filled her with and the possibilities that opened up before she began following Raylan down the ladder. Later, she promised herself, she would deal with whatever this unnameable thing was between them. "Can you see anything?"

"Not yet." Raylan took one more step and then

there was a soft thud as his shoe met packed dirt.
"I hit the bottom, though. It's only about eight feet
down, so watch your step."

She did as he said and stepped off the bottom
rung. Together, Mia and Raylan swung their lights
around the space. Behind them were more concrete
block walls. But in front of them...

In front of them was a long tunnel dug out of the
dirt, supported by a wood frame and strung with
lights that were connected to a switch beside the
ladder. Mia flicked the switch and gasped when the
lights flicked on, one at a time.

"He must have a separate line for these. Probably hooked up to solar panels somewhere. If he was
using this as a panic-room type of thing, that would
make sense because solar would work no matter what
happened."

"Do you think these tunnels come out in the woods?
And maybe that's how Harrington left town?"

"We'll never know unless we look." Raylan put
out a hand. Mia slipped hers into his warm grasp.
"Let's stick together."

"I like that idea." Her wide eyes met his. "Not just
because it's a little eerie down here but because...
well, I like being close to you, even if it's only for
a few minutes."

A goofy grin took over Raylan's face. "I like that,
Mia. I like that a lot."

She answered with a smile of her own. She'd been
kidding herself if she thought she'd ever stopped lov-

ing Raylan. All her earliest memories were of this man who had been both her friend and her first love. They'd been foolish teenagers who couldn't see a future that encompassed both their dreams back in those days. But maybe now, maybe together, they could find a way to make it work. "But let's table what that means for later. Okay?"

"Deal." He held her hand tight, and they moved down the tunnel. They had taken a handful of steps when they heard a scratching sound above them.

Mia froze. "What was that?"

"Maybe a rat? This house has been abandoned for a long time. Stay close."

They made their way farther down the cramped space. The tunnel was about seven feet tall and only four feet wide. Wide enough for one person, but not for the two of them to walk side by side. Mia glanced over her shoulder. Even with the lights above them, they could only see a few feet in either direction. The twin beams of their flashlights, however, offered a wide circle of reassuring light ahead.

Just then Mia's light landed on a pile of dirt a couple feet down the tunnel. "I don't think a rat did that."

When they got closer, they could see that someone had been digging. A shovel was lying on the floor, and the pile of dirt they'd noticed was the first of several that ran down the length of the tunnel. There were holes dug in the floor and walls every few inches, leaving piles of freshly moved earth.

"Someone else has been searching for the money," Raylan said.

"And that means you shouldn't be snooping around," a low, dark voice said from behind them.

Mia tightened her grip on Raylan's hand as the two of them slowly turned around. Raylan reached for the shovel—the only weapon he had—and brought it to his chest. At first, the other man's light was in their eyes, blinding them, but then he lowered the beam, revealing himself.

He was tall, maybe six foot four, with broad shoulders and a heavyset build. He was wearing jeans, a black hooded sweatshirt and a thick camouflage winter coat. He had a rifle in his hands, aimed at Mia. But it was the ski mask that covered his face, revealing only his eyes and his mouth, that was the most terrifying. A ski mask meant he didn't want them to know his identity. A ski mask meant he was up to no good.

Raylan stepped forward, at the same time pulling Mia behind him, protecting her, even here. This close, a bullet could easily go through Raylan and still go into Mia, but she prayed that didn't happen. "Who are you?"

"Doesn't matter who I am because I am the one—" he raised his right hand and racked the rifle with the movement, the sound chilling and terrifying "—with the gun."

Mia wanted Raylan to say it would be okay, but, of course, neither of them knew if that would be true.

They were trapped in a tunnel with a man who had tried to kill them before. They should have told the police they were coming here. They should have waited for backup. They should have made a thousand decisions differently. If Raylan got hurt because of this—

No. She refused to think like that. God was watching over them. Surely, He would provide a way for them to survive this.

"What do you think you two are doing down here?" the man demanded.

"Looking for answers," Mia said. "Like who you are."

Raylan reached back, his hand a note of caution. "We aren't a threat to you."

"Really? Because it sure seemed like those cops have been looking for me for several days and that felt pretty threatening. Because all of you—" he took a step forward, his voice more menacing, his stance angrier "—have been asking way too many questions."

Mia's mind raced, trying to read the man's body language, the hidden meanings beneath his words, looking for a way to make a connection that would make him sympathetic, not murderous. Given that there were millions of dollars at stake—dollars the man had clearly been searching for—Mia wasn't sure that was possible. Greed, she knew, could make ordinary people turn into monsters. "We aren't interested in the money. If that's what you're looking for, we won't get in your way. Just let us go, and we won't tell anyone you are here."

The other man scoffed. "I'm not stupid, so don't even try, lady. I'm not interested in what you have to say." He took another step forward, raising the rifle to eye level as he did and pointing it directly at Mia's chest. "I'm only interested in how *I* am going to make use of *you* to get what I want."

Chapter Ten

Raylan's blood went cold at the sight of that rifle barrel. He wanted to do something—anything—to somehow get them out of this dangerous, possibly deadly, situation. But they were backed into a tunnel, with the only means of escape behind the masked man with the gun. The shovel was useless in his hands unless he could somehow distract the man, get his attention, and his aim, off Mia.

And now the man was advancing on Mia, his gaze on Raylan, but his gun trained on her chest. Raylan gripped the shovel tighter, praying for an opportunity to use it.

"Let her go," Raylan said. "I'll help you instead."

"You?" the man scoffed. "You're just waiting for an opportunity to bash my head in. I'm not stupid. Besides, Mr. Assistant DA, you don't want to be forced to commit a crime, do you? You'll lose that job you love so much."

"I don't care. I'll—"

The man wheeled on Raylan, his eyes dark and glittering with hatred. "You will do what I say, or I will kill this woman. Is that clear?"

Raylan nodded slowly. "Yes."

"Then start backing up. Both of you." He waved the gun at them. "And leave the shovel here."

Raylan bent his knees to drop the shovel, all the while praying for a last-second opportunity, but the man's gaze never wavered, never gave him a flicker of time to react. When the shovel slipped from Raylan's grasp, landing with a soft clunk in the dirt, the fear in Raylan's chest became a tight knot. "I—"

"Shut up!" The man advanced on Raylan in three quick steps, coming face-to-face with him, the rifle poking at Raylan's stomach. "And move. Now."

Raylan and Mia stepped backward, neither of them turning around or giving the man another advantage. They took maybe two dozen steps and then the man said, "Stop." He pointed the rifle at Mia. "You stay here. Your boyfriend is going with me."

Mia glanced at Raylan and then back at the man. "No, please. We'll cooperate, just don't separate us."

The man's gaze narrowed. "Did I ask you to say anything? No. So shut up." He motioned at her pocket. "Give me that key, too. Now!"

Her hand shook as she dug in her pocket, fished out the brass key and then gave it to the man, nodding several times as she did. "Okay, okay. Just promise you won't hurt him."

"The only promise I'll make is that if you try anything, little lady—" the man swiveled the barrel into Raylan's chest "—I'll pull the trigger, and your boyfriend will die. Don't think I won't." He nudged Raylan with the cold metal end. "Now move."

Raylan's heart broke as he kept stepping backward, his gaze locked on Mia's until he and the man rounded a curve, and she disappeared from view. With every step, he looked for a weapon, a way out, anything that could save him from whatever doom was coming for both of them.

But there was nothing.

"Stop and turn around."

Raylan did as he was told because he had no choice. As he pivoted, he saw a door in the side of the tunnel. Reinforced steel with a round handle and a key lock. The panic room that people always suspected Harrington had built. But right now, it looked more like a tomb.

"Open the door," the man said.

Lord, please give me a way out of this. But there was nothing in response, only the heavy, impatient breaths of the man with the gun. Raylan unlocked the door and turned the knob. The door creaked as he pulled it open—steel that likely hadn't been used in more than three decades. On the other side was a small room with a single cot, a pair of lanterns and shelves stocked with emergency rations.

"This is where you die, Mr. Assistant DA." The man gave Raylan a hard shove. Raylan stumbled over the threshold and into the room, landing on his knees on the hard concrete floor. He scrambled to his feet, rushing toward the man. He collided with the stranger in the middle of the doorway, the two of them falling to the ground.

Raylan lunged for the gun. His hand just closed over the barrel, but the man yanked the rifle back at the same time, and the metal slid out of Raylan's grasp.

The man shoved himself up with one hand at the same time Raylan stood up. He prayed that he was moving faster, that he could find another advantage, that he could—

And then the gun went off and sound exploded in the confines of the tunnel. Raylan's head was ringing, his hearing muffled, but he kept moving, fueled by some animal instinct to survive, to protect Mia. He tried to reach for the barrel again, but instead of moving forward, his body fell back, tumbling onto the hard concrete.

The door slammed shut, leaving Raylan in absolute darkness. A second later, he heard the sound of the key turning in the lock, and any hope of escape disappeared.

Mia. The thought flickered in his mind at the same time he realized he was lying in a quickly spreading puddle of sticky, thick liquid. It took a second for him to put it all together, to realize that liquid was his own blood, pouring down the left side of his body. *Oh, God. Please save Mia.*

* * *

As soon as Raylan disappeared around the corner, Mia broke into a sprint, running hard and fast for the ladder that had brought them down into the tunnel. She fished her cell phone out of her pocket as she ran, but one quick glance told her what she already suspected—there was no signal down here, not deep beneath the concrete floor of the basement.

She had just reached for the first rung of the ladder when a loud boom sounded behind her. She paused for a fraction of a second, long enough to hear a slamming noise, to allow the sounds to begin to coalesce in her mind.

A gunshot. A door.

Raylan.

She couldn't save him, not on her own. She needed help. She needed the police. Mia hoisted herself up the first rung of the ladder and was just reaching for the next one when something whizzed past her head, pinging off the metal beside her hand, so close it nicked the side of her finger. Mia's heart thudded in her chest, panic rising up her throat, but she reached for the next rung, lifted her foot and—

The man racked another shot into the chamber. "Stop right where you are, or the next bullet goes in your head."

In a split second, Mia weighed her options. Raylan was back there somewhere, very likely shot, possibly dead—no, she wouldn't think that—and her chances of getting out of here alive had dropped to zero. The man behind her had all the advantages and all the ammunition. No matter how desperately and quickly she climbed, she couldn't outclimb a bullet.

She choked back a sob, hung her head and lowered herself back to the ground.

"I told you not to try anything, missy." The man's voice sounded tighter, darker. The gun in his hand seemed ten times more menacing than before.

Mia covered her head with her hands and whispered prayers under her breath. "Please don't let us die down here. Please protect us. Please, please, please."

The man chuckled. "God isn't coming to get you. But I am. Now get up."

Tears stung the back of Mia's eyes, but she refused to shed them. Refused to let this man see how terrified she was. Was Raylan okay? Where had the man taken him? She'd heard only a heavy thud, something that sounded like a door shutting. But then…nothing.

"Where did you take Raylan?"

"You really don't know when to stop talking, do you?" He waved toward the space in front of him. "Start walking and don't stop until you get to the shovel. And don't waste what few breaths you have left talking to me."

She followed orders and stayed silent as she walked back down the tunnel, but her mind was whirring with questions and worries. Who was this man? How did he know about the tunnel?

What he was looking for was obvious—the money. She had no doubt that his threat to kill them was very, very real. Anyone who would go to such great lengths to find millions of dollars wouldn't want any witnesses left behind.

Mia, who usually had ideas faster than she could speak them aloud, had no idea how to get them out of this situation. She couldn't think of a single word to say or a single move to make that would change the odds.

"Pick up the shovel." His voice was almost a growl.

The weight of the shovel in her hands gave her hope that maybe she could use it against him somehow. Raylan had never had an opportunity, but maybe now with only one of them, the man would let down his guard.

He pressed the muzzle of the gun to her back. "Don't get any ideas."

"What do you want from us?"

"Free labor." He chuckled, the sound disappearing into the thick dirt walls. "Now dig. Right here."

Above the piles of dirt there was a long indentation that ran along the wall, but stopped a few inches in front of her. She could feel the uneven floor beneath her where the man had dug and hastily pushed the dirt back into place. As she looked down the length of the tunnel, she could see similar impressions all up and down the dirt path and walls. "You've been digging all of this up?"

"What did I say about talking? Dig right here." He pointed at a place at chest level on the wall, where he had left off.

"But if you keep digging into the walls, they'll collapse. They're dirt and—"

A hard blow hit the back of her head, and for a second, Mia saw stars. Then a shooting pain ran through her skull, radiating from where he had hit her with the butt of the rifle. She felt dizzy, nauseous, disoriented, but the man didn't care. He shoved the barrel of the gun into her side. "Dig."

She grasped the hard plastic handle of the shovel and began scooping dirt from the wall. Every few scoops, he'd have her stop and drive the blade of the shovel into the space, looking for resistance that would indicate a bag of money or maybe, she feared, a body.

They created a pattern of her digging, then probing, then shuffling forward a few inches and repeating all over again. All the while, Mia worried about Raylan. There was no noise coming from the other side of the tunnel, so she had no idea if he was okay or not. She chose to think that he was, that the man had tied up Raylan, or knocked him out or something, but either way, Raylan would be fine.

If they could get out of here alive.

With every unsuccessful scoop, she could feel the man behind her growing more and more agitated. Clearly, whatever he was expecting to find in these walls wasn't appearing. She had now dug twelve feet down the walls of tunnel, sometimes moving forward, sometimes digging above and below where she'd just dug. The man's instructions seemed to become more and more scattered and frantic as time passed, with nothing showing up in the walls.

A quiet crumbling sound began at the far end of the tunnel, where she had started digging just a half hour earlier. Or maybe it was an hour? She had no idea. Time seemed to both crawl and rush by at a screaming pace down here in the dim light.

She heard dirt skitter down the wall and land in clumps on the floor. The walls were beginning to fall apart, breaking as the holes weakened the structure. Even between the wood supports, she could see the earth beginning to shift and move. She'd read stories of miners buried alive deep in mountains. She didn't want to be one of those people. Every clod of dirt that fell was like a drum beating out the same message—

They didn't have much time before they all died down here.

"If Harrington is dead, then whoever killed him very likely took the money already," Mia said, tentatively, quietly, hoping to manage the delicate balance of distracting him but not rattling him.

"What do you know about Richard Harrington? You never met the man."

"No, but I studied him. I've been researching him for a while, and as much as the police keep saying he ran off to an island somewhere, I just don't believe that's true." He didn't respond, so she kept digging, talking as she did, because talking at least gave her the feeling of doing *something* that could maybe rescue them in the end. "He built this dream house, he had a girlfriend—"

"He abandoned her!" the man interrupted. "Stop talking about him. He deserves to rot, wherever he is."

The word *girlfriend* had clearly struck a nerve. Why? Dolores was dead. Could this man somehow know her, or be related to her? And how could Mia use that to her advantage? "I'm sure that was very difficult for Dolores, to be left alone like that, with no idea where Richard had gone. Even though they'd broken up, I'm sure she worried about him a lot."

"You don't know anything. More digging. No talking."

She did as he said for a while, moving her way down the tunnel, trying not to flinch every time she heard chunks of earth crumbling behind her. It seemed as if the pieces were heavier now, bigger, eroding the structure more and more with each hole she put in the walls. From what she could see, this length of wall was the only side left untouched. There were clear signs the man had been digging into the other side of the wall already and that he had turned over the earth of the entire floor. Maybe this was all one big wild-goose chase for a pot of gold that wasn't going to be found.

She felt the cold, hard muzzle of the rifle in her side. "Faster," he said, his voice a low, dark growl. "We don't have all day."

She swallowed hard and shoved the spade into the

soft earth of the wall. As she did, a huge chunk fell from the dirt ceiling above, crashing onto her head, spraying the two of them with dirt. Mia let out a yelp and tried to jump back, but the gun was still in her side and the man was yelling at her to hurry.

They were all going to die here, entombed in this tunnel.

"The walls are falling apart. Any minute now—"

"I don't care!" The muzzle pressed harder against her side, into the soft space under her rib cage, and all she could think about was how much damage a bullet would do if he pulled that trigger. "Keep digging!"

She shoved the spade in again, hitting only dirt. No suitcase full of money. No bag of thousand-dollar bills. There was nothing in these walls or under the dirt except for more dirt. Every time the head of the shovel sank into the earth, it loosened the unstable wall above, and another hunk fell onto them.

Oh, no! Raylan. If these walls collapsed, not only would Mia and this man die, but Raylan also would. Where was he? Why hadn't she heard his voice? She refused to allow the thought of him dying to even enter her mind. She kept holding on to that whisper of hope that somehow, Raylan was still alive and the two of them would make it out of here.

But as another, even bigger piece of earth crashed to the floor, the hope inside Mia died a little more.

Chapter Eleven

In the pitch-dark, Raylan had to go by feel, and what he felt when he ran his hand down his left side wasn't good. A hole, torn through the top of his arm, not hitting his chest, thank God. He remembered turning slightly at the last second when he tried to reach for the gun. That move had clearly saved his life.

For now, anyway. The shot had gone right through, so he wasn't too worried that the bullet had fragmented inside his body. But it was bleeding heavily, and that wasn't a good sign.

Raylan tore off his T-shirt, tore the fabric in two, then wrapped the stretchy cotton around his left arm, tying it as tight as he could. He winced when pain chased through him. He wrapped the second piece around and knotted it, too. Hopefully, that would be enough to both absorb and stop the bleeding. He got to his feet, moving gingerly, making sure no other parts of his body were hurt.

He estimated that he had been in here for several minutes. Long enough to hear two faint booms a while ago, sounds he told himself were not gunshots. Because if he thought about Mia being wounded—or worse—he would fall apart. Nothing would matter if Mia wasn't okay.

Because he was just as in love with her, if not more so, than he had been twelve years ago. Truth be told, his heart had never let her go. There'd always been this vague hope that somehow, someway, they'd find their way back to each other and it would all end with a sunset and a picket fence.

They had found each other again. But the future he'd dreamed of was never going to happen if he didn't find a way out of here.

His eyes had adjusted a little to the darkness, and he could see a very thin band of light along the seams of the door, coming from the lights in the tunnel. It wasn't enough to see the interior of the room or to make out much more than vague shadows. Raylan closed his eyes and tried to picture the room in his mind. He'd only had the briefest glimpse of the space, not enough to memorize all the details.

He made his way to the door. He felt along the left side for the handle and the dead bolt. There was no key in the lock on this side, but there was a keyhole. Which meant there was a very slim possibility that whoever had built this room had stored a second key inside here, just in case they got locked in.

He began feeling his way around the room, along

the edge of the cot, beneath the bed, between the mattress and the frame. One of the metal poles of the frame was loose enough for Raylan to wriggle it out. It wasn't much for a weapon, but it was better than nothing. He resumed his search for a key.

The shelves were stocked with cases of canned goods, giant plastic tubs of dry goods and packages of toilet paper. He patted the top and bottom of every shelf, then along the metal frame, hoping for a box, a jar, anything that might hold a key. Nothing.

His brain screamed at him to hurry, reminding him of those two booms he'd heard and what they very likely meant.

Racing to finish means you miss the information you need to win, his father used to say. He'd been talking about Raylan's tendency, as an eager young lawyer fresh out of law school, to want to hurry the case along so they could get to court, and the bad guy could be behind bars that much sooner. More than once, his father had said those words to him, and every single time, slowing down had meant Raylan had time to build a stronger case…or uncover evidence that pointed at the true criminal.

His father's advice echoed in his head, a reminder that rushing could mean overlooking the very thing he needed. Raylan forced himself to move slowly and methodically, covering every square inch of a place before moving on to the next. He was just finishing his search of the shelves when he heard rocks and dirt skitter down the steel door. A second shower quickly followed. The earth was giving way. If they didn't get out in time, the tunnel could cave in on them.

Raylan picked up his pace a little, praying as he did that God would help him find the key. More dirt tapped its way down the door, and Raylan was convinced he felt the tunnel shiver.

He had done a complete sweep of the main room. Despair wormed its way into his thoughts. How much time had gone by? Minutes? Hours? The thick steel prevented him from hearing anything in the tunnels, and his mind kept skating down some very dark paths.

Focus. You have to focus.

A tiny bathroom of sorts—really, nothing more than a toilet and a sink—was located in the back corner of the room. There was no light this far back in the space, so Raylan took his time patting down the walls, then opening the vanity and feeling along the pipes. Hot-water line, cold-water line, drainpipe, P trap, remaining drain—

Had the curve of the P trap felt weird? He tried to think back to what the underside of his kitchen sink looked like. He'd repaired a leak a few years ago, but with his dad's help and advice the whole time, which meant Raylan didn't pay super-close attention. He took a breath, calming the urge to rush, and pictured the plumbing in his head.

There should be a connector, then the wider pipe narrowed down to a slightly smaller pipe, which turned into a curve to prevent sewer gases from escaping into the sink, then another set of connectors and finally the main drainpipe.

Raylan ran his hands down the hard PVC piping one more time and hit that same odd ripple. His fingers danced around the shape, and he nearly whooped in relief. There it was, at the back of the pipe—a long, narrow ridge of duct tape that had the distinct outline of a key.

He peeled the tape off the pipe and then removed it from the key. He scrambled to his feet, whacking his head on the underside of the sink as he did, but he barely noticed in his rush to get to the door, find the slot for the dead bolt and, finally, thankfully, insert the key and hear the tumblers release as he turned it.

The walls were crumbling faster with every shovelful of dirt that Mia removed. The structural integrity of the tunnel was failing right before her eyes, but the man with the ski mask didn't seem to care. Even as dirt rained on them from the ceiling and skidded down the walls, he urged her to dig faster and deeper.

Every time she dug in, she prayed she would hit something. That all this could come to a final end. Maybe it would be better to die by rifle blast than by being suffocated under all this earth. For a while, she'd thought that maybe one of her subscribers would notice she hadn't uploaded anything and, in some wild coincidence, call the CVPD and have her rescued. The longer she spent down here, the more improbable the thoughts became. Slowly, the hope she'd held on to for so long ebbed away, and even as she kept praying, she couldn't help but think that maybe this was the ending that God wanted.

"Find it!" the man shouted.

She spun around, exhausted, dirty, aching from her head to her toes. Sweat streamed down her forehead, dripping into her eyes, smearing with the powdery earth on her skin. "How? How exactly am I supposed to find something that might not even be buried here?"

At this point, she didn't care if he shot her. Her arms felt like spaghetti, muscles taxed and weakened, the dirt feeling more like concrete than soft earth. There was dirt covering every inch of her, falling into her hair, gritting inside her shoes. The air down here was becoming thick and humid, the coolness of being below ground slowly disappearing as the tunnel closed in on itself.

The man raised the rifle in one slow deliberate move and aimed it at her head. Mia didn't move. "Don't. Stop. Digging."

There was a sound farther down the tunnel, maybe more of the walls caving in. The path toward the exit was covered in at least six inches of dirt as the earth escaped between the posts and piled up. Soon, the way out would be blocked, and this tunnel would become a tomb.

Mia tossed the shovel onto the ground. "Shoot me then. I'm done digging."

The man let out a scream of frustration. "I'm going to kill you!" He sighted down the long barrel of the rifle, but he was sweating, too, and he couldn't wipe off the sweat under the mask. Finally, he ripped off the ski mask and used it to swipe off the sweat that was pouring down his forehead and into his field of vision.

"I don't care." She was on the verge of tears. They'd been down here so long, and there'd been no sound of Raylan from the other end of the tunnel. He'd undoubtedly been killed by this vicious man, who was definitely going to kill her now, too, because she'd seen his face.

His face. She glanced again at him and the pieces clicked into place. The distinctive curve of his nose, the widow's peak on his forehead.

"You're Harrington's son. Dolores got pregnant before Harrington disappeared, and you're her son."

"I'm the son he *abandoned*, you mean." He leaned in close, spitting his words across her face. Fury flooded his cheeks, sparked in his eyes. "And leaving my mother destitute."

Mia wanted to back away from his rage, but knew that would be perceived as weakness and possibly anger him more. She stood her ground and thought about what she'd seen in her research, looking for something she could use to defuse the situation.

Dolores hadn't been destitute, not that Mia remembered. The house Dolores had lived in had been a nice two-story in a good neighborhood. There'd

been no sign she'd ever filed for bankruptcy or anything like that. She had, however, tried to have Harrington declared dead three different times, but the
court had denied her claims because she was not a
legal relative. A DNA test for her son would have
undoubtedly been impossible without Harrington
himself. That would have left Dolores angry and,
maybe, as she got older, more desperate. A despera-
tion she might have passed on to her son. "And you
think the money is still here? What do you know that
no one else does?"

"I know you're going to die if you don't pick up
that shovel."

Another, bigger hunk of earth fell from the ceiling mere inches from where they were standing, followed by a second and a third. Their time in this
tunnel was quickly coming to an end. "We're both
going to die if I dig up one more inch of soil. Is that
what you want? What your mother would want? All
for some money?"

"That money is mine! It should have been mine
all along! She should have told me about it years ago
so I could have had it! It's mine, not his!" He took
a step forward and pressed the gun into her chest.
His dark gaze locked on hers. Hatred glittered in
his eyes. Mia hadn't mitigated his anger. She'd only
stoked the fire. "So dig."

A flash of something went past her. Mia was
knocked into the side of the tunnel. The gun went off,
a bullet tearing into the ceiling and setting off an av-

alanche of rocks and earth and doom. Mia screamed as the dust and dirt filled the air, her eyes, her lungs. Her head was ringing, and for a moment, she couldn't hear anything. She covered her ears and willed the sharp ringing to stop.

Something yanked at her shirt, then her shoulders, wrapping around her chest, hauling her back, back, back down the tunnel, the cavalcade of loose dirt following like a tsunami. She scrambled with her feet, righting herself and turning, expecting to see Harrington's son's angry face.

Instead, she saw a face she loved with every fiber of her being.

"Raylan!" She grabbed him in a hug, holding him so tight she was sure neither of them could breathe. "You're alive. You're—"

She felt the knot between them. When she looked down, she saw the T-shirt tied around his arm, soaked with crimson. "You're hurt!"

"I'm okay for now." He cupped her face. "But if we don't get out of here, neither of us will be okay."

"But how? The exit is blocked." Behind them, the walls were caving like dominoes, and what had been a few inches of rock and dirt was now a few feet. The path to the ladder was blocked and very likely had caused Dolores's vengeful son's death.

"There's another way out, but we have to go. Now." He took her hand, and they started to run down the tunnel, into a long, dark blackness that swallowed them up.

* * *

When Raylan had first unlocked the door, he'd run right instead of left, maybe disoriented by the darkness or the blood loss, but that mistake had sent him into a dirt wall. When he ran into it, some of the earth came loose, revealing another ladder. The other end of the tunnel, just as he'd suspected. And what he prayed was a way out.

Then he'd heard the man yelling at Mia, and he spun toward her, overriding his instincts to escape, to save himself. Not if Mia was in danger. Nothing came before Mia's life. As Raylan had turned the corner, he'd taken in everything in a fast second— the gun, the falling earth, the man's anger. Raylan had raised the metal piece from the bed and hit the man at the same time the gun went off, firing into the ceiling and releasing an avalanche. Then Raylan had lunged for Mia, just in time to catch the edge of her shirt and then the rest of her.

God had been there, of that Raylan had no doubt, helping him reach Mia in time and get them both out of the worst of it. But they weren't safe yet. Behind them, he could hear the wood supports creaking and straining, see the pebbles of dirt coming down like a waterfall on the sides of the tunnel, and he knew it would only be a matter of seconds before the rest caved in.

"Go up, Mia. Climb."

She glanced up the path. "But the trapdoor is closed. What if it's locked?"

"We'll deal with that when we get there." Rocks and thick, dense clods of earth pounded down onto the floor, making the entire tunnel shake and groan. "Climb!"

Mia scrambled up the ladder and pushed at the trapdoor. "Raylan! It won't move!"

"You can't get away!" Harrington's son yelled, a bloodcurdling scream of rage, followed by the unmistakable and terrifying echo of a bullet exploding out of the gun.

Raylan kept moving, up the ladder, right beside Mia. "We'll have to push together." A second shot rang out, slamming into the ladder, spraying them with shards of metal.

Raylan could see the terror in Mia's eyes, feel it in the tension of her body so close to his. "We can do this," he said, with far more confidence than he felt. "On three?"

A third shot pinged off the ladder, higher this time, and the man's voice was closer, nearly below them.

"Better make it on one."

"One!" Raylan shouted, and they both slammed their shoulders into the hatch.

"Got you!" the man said.

Raylan had a terrifying glimpse of the dark, lethal barrel of the rifle and then the hatch opened, and he and Mia scrambled out of the tunnel, onto the grass and into a thunderstorm. An angry rumble sounded below them just as the tunnel collapsed into itself, taking the man and his gun with it.

Raylan had no idea if Harrington's son could have survived. He wasn't going to take that chance.

"Run!" Raylan grabbed Mia's hand, and they started running, their feet slipping on the slick, wet grass. They ran and ran and ran until they reached the carriage house. "Get in the house. Call the cops. I'm going to go back and look for him."

"Raylan, no—"

But it was too late. He had already turned back toward the widening hole in the ground. He grabbed a branch from the ground to serve as a weapon as he ran, raising it over his shoulder. He skidded to a stop. There was nothing to fight. Only a burial mound of dirt.

Chapter Twelve

It took the Crooked Valley Police Department a solid day to bring in the heavy equipment and dig down deep enough to recover Harrington's son's body. He'd been named Joseph, the birth records said. With no proof of Harrington being the parent, Dolores had named him Rouse, which had surely kept anyone from putting the pieces together about his identity. After the police removed Joseph, it took another couple of hours to carefully excavate the rest, including the panic room.

After they had been looked over and patched up by EMTs, and then given their statements to the police, Mia and Raylan were allowed to watch as the workers hauled out the dirt and the forensics team began searching. Grandpa Louis had come to the crime scene, too, but Hugh had held him back, still holding firm to his belief that Louis Beaumont was involved somehow.

"He's not involved, Hugh," Raylan said. "I have a strong feeling that what we find here will prove that."

Mia gave Raylan's hand a squeeze. It made her feel less alone to know Raylan was on her side and protecting her grandfather as much as she was.

Hugh assessed his assistant DA for a long time. "You're as great, if not better, an attorney as your father, Raylan. You have good instincts. And you were far closer—too close, considering you almost died—to this case than I was. If you believe that in your gut…"

"I do, sir. I truly do. Let me walk you through what I know so far." Raylan put the pieces together for Hugh, creating a timeline and motive based on what they had learned over the last two weeks. Hugh listened and nodded from time to time. It wasn't until Raylan finished that the skepticism finally disappeared from his eyes.

"I'll allow Beaumont to be here. But if we find anything—"

"You won't."

"It'll be your career on the line, not mine." Hugh waved at the cop to allow Louis through. "Don't make me regret this, Raylan."

There was a yawning screech as the excavator peeled up the roof of the panic room, exposing the floor plan. Just as Raylan had described, there was not much. A bathroom. A cot. Shelves. Supplies.

Louis came to stand beside them, his face somber yet curious. It was an odd situation, watching the police unearth decades of secrets. Bringing them into the light, as Raylan had said. The one thing Dolores had despised. It all made sense now, Mia thought.

"It was pitch-black when I was in that panic room," Raylan said to Mia. "It seemed so terrifying. But now it looks like nothing more than a big closet."

The metal roof let out one last groan as the machines folded the roof onto itself as easily as folding a piece of paper. As they did, sunlight exposed the one thing Raylan hadn't discovered.

A skeleton, curled into the far corner of the bathroom, tucked into the corner of the shower, hidden behind a plastic shower curtain. A pistol was lying at his feet. Grandpa Louis grabbed Mia's hand. "That's Richard."

"How do you know?"

Grandpa Louis pointed at something glinting on the concrete floor. "The watch. I can't tell for sure from this far away, but I'm positive that's Richard's Rolex. I always thought it was big and gaudy and too glittery, but he loved that thing and wore it every single day."

Raylan crossed to the cops and his boss and conferred with them as the forensics team dropped into the room and began examining the body. A few minutes later, Raylan nodded and then walked back to the group.

"It is a Rolex, and given the fact that there aren't a lot of people in this small town with that kind of watch, it looks like you were right, Louis," Raylan said. "But we still don't know why Harrington took the money or where it is."

Grandpa Louis shrugged. "Greed. I wouldn't have thought it of him, but I don't see any other explanation."

Mia watched the coroner and the forensics team work the panic room. The excavator was moved back, and all the workers were ordered off-site while the team went through every inch of what had now become a new crime scene. The body in the shower was left undisturbed while the coroner did his assessment. It would be a while before they lifted it out and had any more information on a cause of death.

Mia thought about everything she had read and seen and all the pieces of the mystery that had been scattered in her mind. She turned to Raylan. "Do you still have that article where Dolores was interviewed?"

He nodded. "I have a printout of it in my car. I brought the file home to go over tonight."

"How do you feel about going over it right now?" She shot him a smile, and when he smiled in return, her heart fluttered a bit. "And let's call Eddie and get his take."

"I don't think it's time for an exclusive interview yet. We still need to positively ID the body." Raylan considered her for a moment. "But if you trust him, then I do, too."

"Eddie seems like a good guy. I think he'll work with us." Mia took out her phone and called the reporter. The day she'd talked to him, she'd put his contact info into her address book, thinking it might come in handy someday.

The three of them decided to go to Cappy's Diner and leave the police the space they needed to do their job. Even though he was clearly tired from standing in the cold and watching the police, Grandpa Louis insisted on coming with them. Mia knew how much solving this mystery meant to him, so she agreed, with reluctance, because she didn't want her already weak grandfather to suffer a health setback.

They took a big table in the back a few feet away from the booth where Raylan and Mia had always sat. She glanced over at Raylan as Cappy handed them menus and caught him eyeing "their" booth, too, with what looked like wistfulness.

That was something she would have to deal with later because Raylan had started spreading the research about Dolores across the table. Mia took her notebook out of her tote bag and paired her research with his. While they waited for Eddie to arrive, the three of them took turns reading the articles, scanning the property records and all the other scraps of information about Dolores. In the wake of what her son had done, every piece of data looked different.

"Joseph said she was destitute, but she wasn't." Mia pointed to the real-estate valuation for her three-bedroom Colonial-style house. "Maybe he has a different interpretation of poor than the rest of the world does."

"You know, I've been spending a lot of time trying to remember if Richard ever talked about Dolores," Grandpa Louis said. "After you asked me about Richard's girlfriend, I started thinking back. He and I never really talked about our personal lives much, but I remembered a conversation we had shortly before he disappeared. He came into the office, and he was clearly stressed and angry. Richard was usually a pretty even-keeled guy, but this day he wasn't. I asked him what was bothering him, and he said it was trouble with a woman."

"Dolores?"

Louis shrugged. "He never said her name, but I'm thinking maybe it was her."

Mia shuffled the printouts around until she found the one she wanted. The interview with Eddie that Dolores had given a few years before her death. The one where she'd been labeled a crackpot, obsessed with the past. Obsessed, Mia believed, with finding the money, with uncovering the secrets she had alluded to. How far would someone go? Far enough to kill?

"Hey, what'd I miss?" Eddie said as he walked up to them.

Raylan gestured to the seat beside Grandpa. "Quite a lot, it turns out. We don't have all the answers yet, but if you work with us, I promise to give you an exclusive when we break the news about Harrington." He gave Eddie a rough overview of what had transpired in the last twenty-four hours. "So far, we've been able to keep the media off the property, but that won't last long."

"And you want to solve the mystery before someone else does." Eddie thought about it for a second. "That sounds fair. Mind if I take notes?"

"Not at all."

Mia turned the article about Dolores toward Eddie. "What was your impression of her? In the piece, you call her obsessed."

Eddie scoffed. "Obsessed would be putting it mildly. Dolores could talk about nothing else, at least when her husband wasn't in the room. The second he left for work, she unloaded about how much she hated Harrington for, and I quote, 'ruining her life.'"

"Why didn't you put all that in the article?" Grandpa Louis paused when Cappy came over with drinks and burgers, and the three of them cleared space for the food.

"Looks like some serious thinking is going on here," Cappy said.

"Is there another kind?" Grandpa grinned at his old friend. "Thanks for the food, Cap."

"On the house." Cappy's eyes teared up as he glanced at Mia and then Raylan. "I'm just glad you two are okay. That everyone is safe."

Raylan reached across the table and gave Mia's hand a squeeze. "We are, too."

She wanted to ask him about that, but then Cappy exchanged a little small talk with her grandfather and Raylan released her, and the four of them started eating. There never seemed to be a good time to say, *What's going on between us? Are you feeling what I'm feeling? Or is this just an after-nearly-dying rush of gratitude?*

Eddie picked a fry out of the plate the four of them opted to share. "My editor was the reason none of that made it into the article," he said, drawing Mia's attention back to the mystery. "Most of what Dolores said couldn't be verified so I kept the article pretty lean, and even then, my editor cut out half of what I wrote."

Mia leaned across the table. "What got cut?"

"Well, between you and me, I think Dolores was stalking Richard. She talked about being on his property a lot and being angry that she saw him meeting with another, younger woman."

"Danielle." Grandpa Louis shook his head and his eyes teared up. "She went to Richard's house to drop off some paperwork before she and Paul went out of town. Only they never left."

"Those are the bodies you guys found?" Eddie asked.

Raylan nodded. "So that puts Dolores on the property at or around the same time they died. We found a woman's belongings in the carriage house. If Dolores was hiding out there to spy on Harrington, those would be her clothes."

"Makes sense," Mia said. "I doubt Richard ever went out to the guesthouse. If he didn't know he had a guest, he wouldn't have any reason to check it."

"Dolores talked about breaking into Richard's office," Eddie added. "Trying to get the money he owed her. She was, like I said in the article, *obsessed*."

"Maybe that's because…" Raylan turned his phone toward the group and showed them a birth certificate that Mia could see had just been emailed by Morales. "Joseph was born only a month after she got married to the insurance agent, and about six months after Harrington disappeared."

"So Dolores finds out she's pregnant after they break up," Mia said, "and wants Harrington to support the baby, but he wants nothing more to do with her. Maybe he made her even madder by suggesting the baby wasn't his. They had been broken up for a few months, after all."

"And maybe to make her go away, he gives her that hundred thousand dollars he withdrew shortly before he disappeared," Grandpa Louis added. "Thinking that would take care of it."

"But it wasn't enough," Eddie continued. "She wanted it all. I could tell, just talking to her, that she thought he owed her big-time."

"And if she was snooping in his home office, maybe she found out how to log in to the bank accounts to steal the money he wouldn't give her." Raylan turned to Louis. "Is that where he kept the bank information? At the home office?"

"There and at work. Just so he could always access what he needed." Grandpa shook his head. "And I bet she broke in the night of September thirtieth."

"How do you know the exact date?" Raylan asked.

"Fiscal quarters." Grandpa looked at Mia and Raylan. "Fiscal quarters end every three months—March thirty-first, June thirtieth, September thirtieth, December thirty-first. Richard and I used to sit down on the last day of the quarter and look at the company's performance. Was it up, was it down, had we done poorly in this area or that? I remember we had had a fabulous quarter that September. One of our best ever. Richard and I had even talked about going out to lunch the next day to celebrate. He came in early the morning of October first, and by the time I got there, I saw that his office was a mess and Richard was flustered and angry. He was muttering something about his home office and losing a piece of paper. I had no idea that piece of paper was his bank information."

"So he didn't tell you that someone had been in his home office?" Mia asked.

Grandpa shook his head. "Richard disappeared a few days later. I had no idea. I didn't make the connection that those things went together. Like I said, Richard was very private and didn't share much of anything about his personal life. Richard had become more and more paranoid in the months before he disappeared, and after everything that happened, I was convinced he *was* hiding the money, because of the Feds looking into his practices. It all makes sense. The SEC investigation, Dolores… It would make a man who was already suspicious become very suspicious. I bet he withdrew the money to keep her from getting it, especially if he realized she had found the bank-account information and was planning to withdraw it herself."

Raylan nodded. "And the cops didn't put it together because everyone thought he was living on some private island, spending the money on margaritas. It wasn't until years passed that the police began to suspect he might be dead."

"And by then, Dolores was a distant memory," Mia added.

"Especially if no one was tying them together because very few people knew they had even dated. And she seemed so quiet and ordinary, not at all like a murderer."

Grandpa Louis shook his head. "I wish I had known more or thought of Dolores when the police first questioned me. Maybe all of this could have been avoided."

Mia covered her grandfather's hand with her own. "You didn't even know her name, Grandpa. There wasn't much you could have told them. And you were undoubtedly very upset because the money was gone."

"You have no idea. Clients were calling all hours of the day. Some were angry, and some were crying. Their life savings, gone. Their retirement, gone. They were devastated and scared."

"And so were you." Mia gave him a sympathetic smile. "You did the best you could at the time."

"Maybe I did." Her grandfather sighed. "Maybe I did."

Raylan's phone buzzed with a text message. "It's

Morales. Says he has some information he wants to share. Is it okay if I just have him meet us here?"

"Yes, yes, of course." Did this mean that Raylan was 100 percent convinced of her grandfather's innocence? Mia started to ask that very question and stopped herself. If the answer was no, that might stress Grandpa Louis out, and the last thing she wanted was for him to worry.

A few minutes later, the detective strode into the diner. He gave Cappy a nod, waved off the offer of food and headed straight for the table where Mia, Raylan, Eddie and Louis were sitting. Their dishes had been cleared away, and they had gone back to reading the contents of the file while they exchanged their own theories about the case. Mia tapped Raylan's hand. "Morales is here."

"Hey there." The detective flipped a chair around and sat at the end of the booth. He glanced at the ADA and then nodded toward the rest of them. "Are you sure you want them present?"

Raylan glanced at Eddie. "You can trust me," the reporter said. "I can keep this under wraps for a little while."

Louis and Mia both nodded. Raylan gave Mia a smile and turned back to the detective. "Yes, I'm sure."

"Okay. Works for me." Morales waved between the four of them. "I've already talked to Hugh, and he gave me the okay to talk to you and Mia, and you, Louis. However, this is an ongoing investigation so none of this leaves this table until we make an official statement, which should happen in about an hour." He took a deep breath, then looked between Louis and Mia. "I wanted to come here in person first to tell you that your grandfather is officially cleared as a suspect."

A tidal wave of relief ran through Mia. "Really? Are you sure?"

Morales nodded. "What we found at the scene tells us that. Literally." He took out his phone and opened the photos app, then turned the screen so that the others could see it. Behind the body was a metal panel that had been opened. Inside was a thick bag filled with money. "Harrington had the money with him, as we suspected, but he also had a rather lengthy note in his pocket. There was an envelope addressed to you, Louis, that I think he was planning to drop off or mail after he got away."

"So he *was* robbing the company and clients." Grandpa seemed on the verge of tears. "I never thought he had it in him."

"Not exactly." Morales pinched the screen and expanded the image so they could read parts of the letter. "He explains what happened here and what his plan was."

Mia read the words aloud, the answers they had sought for so long finally coming to light.

"Dolores came to the house this morning to demand more money from me. Danielle and her husband were there, stopping by to say goodbye before they headed out of town. Dolores had a gun, and before I could call the police, she shot Danielle. She made me tie up Paul and told me to come back with the money or she'd kill them both. She was enraged, Louis, and there was nothing I could do to stop her. She told me that if she saw the police pull up, she'd kill me, too. Louis, I didn't know what to do. I was so scared. I withdrew the money, but I'm not giving it to her. I'm going to get the revolver out of the panic room and go after Dolores. Forgive me."

Mia glanced up at Morales. "That's the end of the letter."

He nodded somberly. "Harrington never got a chance to leave the panic room. He was shot by Dolores and locked inside. She killed Danielle and Paul, too, but there's no way of knowing if they died before or after Harrington did."

"What about the money?"

"Harrington had stashed it in a wall, just as Joseph had suspected, but not in the tunnels themselves. Harrington had installed a safe in the walls of the panic room and hidden it behind the shelves, just as he'd hidden the tunnel beneath shelves. We found it there as we took the panic room apart to get to the body. It was pretty well concealed. We think that hiding space is where Harrington kept the gun."

"And when he went to get the gun, he hid the money.

Dolores maybe got angry, thinking he didn't have the money, and she shot him, then locked the door," Mia said. "What a way for Harrington to die."

"So he's been there, all this time. Him and the money." Grandpa shook his head. "That's so sad."

Morales nodded again. "The bullets that we found in Danielle and Paul and in Harrington all match. They aren't the same caliber as Harrington's gun, so we're pretty sure they came from Dolores's gun."

Mia sighed. "But she's dead, so you'll never know."

"Actually, we do know. Joseph had the rifle in the tunnel, but he also had a pistol in his truck. Dolores's pistol, we believe. She never registered it, but it was clearly an old pistol, small and light, the kind a woman would have. And it was engraved with her initials. Maybe a gift from Harrington himself, but we'll never know. We're pretty confident it's the same weapon that killed everyone else. Once we have the ballistics report back, we'll be sure." Morales glanced at Raylan and Mia. "You two narrowly missed being killed. You should have called me. It's amazing that you survived."

Raylan took Mia's hand in his own, and a smile spread across his face. "It is. And it's one I'll be thanking God for the rest of my life."

Raylan stayed behind with Eddie to give him that exclusive interview he'd promised. Mia brought Grandpa Louis home and got him settled in his favorite chair. He went to bed early to get some much-deserved sleep while she uploaded the latest episode of her show. She'd create one more in a week or so to wrap everything up. So far, this going-home series had garnered more views than any of her previous shows. Her channel was climbing the ranks of You-Tube a little more each hour. This was a good thing for her show and for its ability to get the word out about all the victims she hadn't found and all the cases she hadn't yet solved. Except the success she'd worked to achieve for so long didn't fill her with the elation she'd expected it would.

The next afternoon, Mia was making her grand-father a cup of tea and rustling around in his cabi-nets. "What do you want for dinner? I think there's enough here to make chili. Or I can order a pizza or—"

"Or you can go have dinner with the man you're in love with."

Mia shut the cabinet door and stared at her grand-father. "What did you just say?"

"You heard me, stubborn granddaughter." Grandpa gave her a tender smile. "You've been in love with that boy almost as long as you've known him. Don't be so scared that you let him slip away and run off to New York again."

"I live in New York, Grandpa. I work there."

He waved that off. "You can do that show of yours from anywhere in the country. Why, you just did an episode right here. And you could do every epi-

sode going forward from right here, if you're brave
enough."

"I think I'm pretty brave. I just tangled with a murderer."

"That's a different kind of brave, my dear Mia.
Be brave with your heart, not just your head." Her
grandfather shooed her out of the room, pressing her
jacket and keys into her hands as he did. She stam-
mered protests, but he wouldn't hear them. "I'm just
as capable of ordering a pizza as you are. Now go."

She went out to her car, fully intending to go to
Julia's or Chloe's instead of Raylan's. No matter
what Grandpa thought, her life was in New York.
But her car had other ideas, and when she tried to
steer west, she found herself heading east, down a
familiar street where a familiar man lived. As she
pulled into his driveway, she saw that he was just
getting into his car.

She rolled down her window, trying to keep the
rising tide of disappointment stuffed inside her.
"Sorry, I didn't know you were going out."

He grinned and pocketed his keys as he crossed to
her car. "Don't be sorry. You saved me a trip. I was
coming to see you."

"You were?" Her breath caught, but she kept that
little bird of hope tightly tamed in her chest. "Why?"

He opened her car door, waited for her to unfasten
her seat belt and then helped her out. She stepped to
the side while he shut the door. His gaze never left
hers. It was a cold wintry day, but Mia didn't feel

anything but the warmth of Raylan's gaze. "That's better."

"For what?"

"This." He leaned down and kissed her.

When Mia raised her gaze to Raylan's, a dozen years disappeared in a blink. He'd seen that look a hundred times, from the day Susan had started baby-sitting the Beaumont girls and he'd made fast friends with Mia. *Raylan, can you help me make a snack? Raylan, can you help me with this math problem?* And later when they were teenagers who fell madly in love—*Raylan...will you kiss me, please?*

She had been his first and best kiss, and the only kiss that stayed in his mind for more than a decade. He'd loved Mia Beaumont all his life, and knew he always would. The only question was whether she loved him back.

He pulled back from her and took her hands in his own. "We've been a little busy the last couple of days—"

"Running from a murderer, solving a crime." She shrugged. "I wouldn't call that busy."

Raylan chuckled. Laughing hurt a little because it aggravated the healing hole in his arm, but as long as he was laughing with Mia, the pain was far easier to bear. "And so I haven't had a chance to tell you what I should have told you twelve years ago."

She opened her mouth to speak, but he put a finger over her lips, afraid to let her negate it, afraid to let the magic disappear before he got the words out.

"I love you, Mia Beaumont. I have loved you my entire life. And if New York is where your life is, then New York is where my life is, because all I ever want is for you to be by my side for the rest of my life, starting right now."

Mia shook her head and Raylan's heart sank. "Your life is not in New York, Raylan."

"Mia—"

Now it was her turn to shush him with a fingertip. "Because my life isn't there anymore. It's right here, with the mountains and the snow and my family. And you." She raised her gaze to his. Her eyes danced with merriment and something more. "Because I still love you, too."

They were words he'd waited so long to hear. Words that filled him with a joy he couldn't describe, a gratitude he would always have.

"I'm so glad, Mia. So incredibly glad." Then he leaned in and kissed her again, and just like that, Raylan was eighteen again and in love with a girl who was running fast in the opposite direction, and wondering how his heart would ever recover from her leaving. This time, she stayed put, and everything he had ever dreamed of came true while the snow danced in the air around them.

Epilogue

Spring in Crooked Valley was alive with possibilities and hope. Raylan and Mia sat on the back porch of Grandpa Louis's house, planning their wedding, while Julia and Chloe helped set up for dinner. Their babies sat in a playpen together, cooing and laughing over the same toys.

"We'll have to hurry up," Mia said to Raylan.

He hardly glanced up from the brochure he was looking at for a wedding chapel. "Hurry up what?"

"Having a baby. So that he or she gets to grow up with cousins that are around the same age."

Raylan's eyes widened in surprise and then happiness. He took her hand in his and held it tight. "I can't think of anything I want more. But let's get married first, Miss Always Running Fast."

She laughed. "There's a lot of life I want to experience, Raylan Westfield. I don't want to sit on the sidelines."

"I will never ask you to sit on the sidelines." He leaned over to give her a quick kiss. "But let's at least do one thing at a time. We just solved a big mystery."

"And I'm ready to solve my next one. With my husband-to-be's help, of course." She grinned at him. They'd made quite the team working on the Harrington case, and as she looked at the next cold case she wanted to take on—the disappearance of a young woman in a town near Crooked Valley five years ago—she could think of no better partner in crime than Raylan.

The ending of this mystery had been bittersweet and yet a cause for joy in other ways. Hugh had agreed to release the money from evidence, since they couldn't prosecute Dolores for Harrington's death. Grandpa Louis dug out his old records and divided every dime between the families that had lost their money when Harrington disappeared. Even though Mia told him he should keep some for himself, he told her he already had all the blessings he needed with his granddaughters. Finally, after Mia's insistence, he kept a small amount, a fraction of what he had lost when Harrington disappeared.

Raylan had spent a long afternoon at the memory care unit, telling his father about the entire case. Mia had come along, for moral support and to visit with the man who had raised such a wonderful son. There were moments when it seemed like his father wasn't listening, and Raylan got ready to leave, frustration all over his face. Just as Raylan stood, his father reached out, grabbed his hand and gave it a squeeze. A small smile crossed his face. "Thank you." Whether he was thanking Raylan for the visit or for closing the case, they'd never know, but Mia was pretty sure it was for bringing an old man some much-needed closure. Something every one of them had deserved for many years.

Grandpa Louis came out to the porch, carrying a big bowl of potato salad. He waved off his granddaughter's attempts to take it from him. "I have been in remission for five months. I am fine. You all can stop worrying about me."

Julia chuckled. "That will never happen, Grandpa. Besides, I have to worry about you, now that I stopped worrying about Mia." She drew her sister into a one-armed hug and then leaned down to whisper in Mia's ear. "I am so happy for you. And so happy you are staying in Crooked Valley."

Tears sprang to Mia's eyes, but instead of wiping them away, she let them fall. She had her family, she had love and hope, and that was all that mattered. Her relationship with her sisters had grown stronger in the last few months, especially because they saw each other nearly every day. Mia had made the coffee shop her de facto office, and the three girls often talked about the cases over a cup of cappuccino in the afternoons. It was…wonderful. "Me, too, Julia."

The three couples sat down around the big table that Grandpa had bought to fit his expanding family, especially now that they were all visiting regularly. Grandpa had started going out more often, seeing his friends and even getting friendly with a widow down the street. His color was back, and the happy grandfather they all remembered had replaced the one who had been beaten down by suspicion for three decades.

"I have an announcement." Grandpa got to his feet and put a hand on Raylan's shoulder. "Actually, it's one that Raylan and I have together."

Mia glanced at her fiancé. "You didn't tell me anything about this."

"Some things are meant to be a surprise." He pressed a kiss to her cheek. "Louis, I'll let you do the honors."

Grandpa cleared his throat. "The Harrington mansion has been sold. To myself and Raylan. We used my portion of the money that was recovered when Harrington's body was found to buy it from the town. We convinced them to sell it for nothing more than the back taxes because it was in such bad shape. Raylan and I are planning on renovating it and making it into a shelter for victims of domestic abuse. Well, not renovating it ourselves. Hiring some local contractors to do that, since I'm retired and Raylan's pretty busy convicting criminals and marrying Mia." Grandpa looked down at his granddaughter and gave her a loving smile. "So that no one ever has to be locked in a situation that puts their lives at risk ever again."

Everything that Mia had been driven by, every case she had worked so hard to solve, was now coming back tenfold. All those women whose stories she had told…and now, maybe, this house would mean some stories would never have to be told because the women would be safe from harm. Mia burst into tears, telling herself she was just overwhelmed by all the togetherness and wedding plans. "Oh, Grandpa, that is so wonderful. And Raylan…" She just shook her head because the words got caught in her throat.

"I know, Mia. I know." He wrapped an arm around her, and the two of them watched the sun begin to set just beyond the mountains. "You've changed my life. Let's change the lives of the women in this valley."

She couldn't think of a better mission to have: speaking for the voices of the past while also helping the voices of the present. "That's a tall order, Mr. Westfield. But I'm up for the challenge, as long as you're by my side."

"There is nowhere in the world I'd rather be, my love." Mia sighed and settled against his side. The sun descended behind the mountains, kissing the valley one last time with gold, and leaving a touch of magic in its wake.

* * * * *